'The horse now lifted its head and neighed softly, and Joe, going to him, stroked his muzzle and said, "There, there, it's all right, boy. It's all right." Then looking up into his face he said firmly, "I'm going to tell you something. I'm more determined now than ever to keep you. I don't care what they say, any of 'em, me mam or dad, or Mr Billings, or that fool just gone, "I'm goin' to keep you, so don't worry your head, lad. Don't worry your head."

The Gladiator now muzzled him and made the sound that he used to make to Mr Prodhurst and it warmed Joe. As there was no-one to see him he put his face against the horse's cheek and whispered, "No matter what you look like, you're mine." '

An unlikely friendship with an old rag-and-bone man, Mr Prodhurst, leads fifteen-year-old Joe Darling into the greatest challenge of his life. For Mr Prodhurst bequeaths his peculiar-looking horse, The Gladiator, to Joe. But how can Joe possibly look after the horse properly? He is determined to try . . .

**Also available by Catherine Cookson,
and published by Corgi Books:**

# CATHERINE COOKSON

## JOE AND THE GLADIATOR

**CORGI BOOKS**

# JOE AND THE GLADIATOR

## A CORGI BOOK 0 552 526177

First published by Macdonald 1968

PRINTING HISTORY
Corgi edition published 1990

*Conditions of sale*
1. This book is sold subject to the condition that it shall
not, by way of trade *or otherwise,* be lent, re-sold, hired
out or otherwise circulated, without the publisher's prior
consent in any form of binding or cover other than that in
which it is published *and without a similar condition
including this condition being imposed on the subsequent
purchaser.*
2. This book is sold subject to the Standard Conditions of
Sale of Net Books and may not be re-sold in the UK below
the net price fixed by the publishers for the book.

This book is set in 11/12 pt Century Textbook
by Colset Private Limited, Singapore.

Corgi Books are published by Transworld Publishers Ltd.,
61–63 Uxbridge Road, Ealing, London W5 5SA, in
Australia by Transworld Publishers (Australia) Pty. Ltd.,
15–23 Helles Avenue, Moorebank, NSW 2170, and in
New Zealand by Transworld Publishers (N.Z.) Ltd., Cnr.
Moselle and Waipareira Avenues, Henderson, Auckland.

Made and printed in Great Britain by
Hazell Books Ltd
Aylesbury, Bucks, England
Member of BPCC Ltd

To all children who make animals their concern
I dedicate *Joe and The Gladiator*

# One

Joe Darling rose from the table and put his top coat and scarf on, then he went and stood near his mother for a moment and looked hard at her, and she put her hand on his shoulder and smiled at him as she said, 'Don't worry; it'll pan out. Things usually do.' He bit on his lip, before turning from her and going out into the chill dark morning.

Doors were opening and closing on both sides of the street and voices commenting on the weather came to him, muffled through the chilling gloom as he made his way out of Mabel Street, cut across Railway Street and into Templetown Road, which led to the shipyards.

At a point along this road Joe usually met up with his pal, Willie Styles, but this morning he had reached the end of the road and was almost at the yard gates and Willie hadn't put in an appearance.

He stopped for a moment and looked back, thinking. Well, I'm not going to wait for him again; I'll only be late and get it in the neck. I've told him afore. But even so he didn't go towards the gates for some minutes, and it was just as he was about to continue on his way that the lanky form of Willie came racing through the lifting gloom towards him.

'By! you've just made it by the skin of your teeth.'

Willie fell into step beside him, panting so hard for a moment that he couldn't speak, and then on a laugh he stammered, 'Y ... you know somethin'? I wish I was back at school. I do, honest Injun.'

'You must be daft.'

'Aye, very likely, b ... but I'd rather be daft and sleep until eight than be sa ... sane and get up at seven.'

'Well the morrow you don't have to stay till nine when we go to the Tech.'

'Oh lor! that's worse. You know, man, I wish I'd never gone in for it. I can't see very much future in marine plumbing, not for me any road.'

'You haven't given it a chance yet, you've only been on it six weeks.'

'It seems like six years.'

'You mean to say you don't like going to the Tech either, I thought you did?'

'Aw, I did at first, but it gets on me wick.'

'But you said you wished you were back at school.'

'Aye, I did, but that's different.'

'Aye, it's different,' laughed Joe; 'You've got to use your brains now.'

'Brains!' said Willie scornfully. 'And what do we do with our brain work when we get back on the job? Carry pipes from A to B, push the said pipes through hole D an' don't look surprised if it pops out in either X, Y or Z.'

For the moment Joe forgot the feeling that

pervaded his home, he forgot that deep inside he was miserable, and as he burst out laughing he pushed his lanky companion and said, 'You'll come popping up through X, Y, Z, one of these days and Mr Ripley'll be waiting for you up top with a flannel hammer.'

Willie, his face one wide grin now, said, 'I don't care who hits me with a flannel hammer as long as it's not Harry Farthing. Lor, I'm tellin' you Joe, if he keeps on at me I'll belt him one. See if I don't.'

'Don't be daft. He'll knock you into the middle of next week.'

'Just let him try it on, that's all.'

Joe wasn't worried about what Willie might do to Harry Farthing. If Harry Farthing said, 'Jump to it!' Willie would jump to it. Willie was all talk. He always had been. All the time they had been at school together Willie had threatened what he was going to do to this one and that one, but when it came to the point Willie did nothing, because he was a coward.

There had been three of them at school, he and Willie and Matty Doolin. He wished Matty was still with them, but he was now working happily on a farm in the wilds of Northumberland. Funny how that had come about, all through them going camping. He often thought of Matty; Matty was a different kettle of fish altogether from Willie. Willie was fun, you could always get a laugh with Willie, but he doubted if Willie would stand by you in a tight corner, more likely to joke his way out of it and leave you to carry the can. Oh, he knew Willie, but still he couldn't help liking him.

When they reached the ship they were working

9

on, Willie went first, making great play of dashing up the ladder and nearly falling flat on his face when he reached the deck.

Six weeks ago Joe had been bewildered by the apparent chaos he found below decks, particularly in the section to which he had been allocated, and for the first two or three days he didn't know whether he was coming or going, or whom to take orders from, until Mr Jack Ripley made it plain to both him and Willie, and also to the third apprentice, Roddy Canner, that he was the boss, and if they wanted to know anything they had to come to him.

There were about fifteen men working on the section and he got on well with all of them, except Harry Farthing. Harry Farthing, in a way, was an apprentice like themselves but he didn't go to the Technical College, nor was he studying for exams. Why this was so Joe couldn't fully understand, because he seemed to know his job, at least he talked as if he did, but then again only when Mr Ripley or the older men weren't about. Harry Farthing was nineteen and already seemed a man to Joe because of his height and bulk. Joe wasn't exactly frightened of Harry Farthing but he wished that circumstances had been such that Farthing was working in some other part of the ship.

But Harry Farthing wasn't working in some other part of the ship and he greeted the two boys with, 'Ah! the college students. An' strike me if they're not wearing their college scarves.'

'You're kiddin',' said Willie. 'This isn't a college scarf, I've had it for years. But we can wear the college scarves, and the badges an' all if we want. There's a smasher, all g . . . gold . . .'

'No kiddin'?' Harry Farthing's voice was awe-filled, and Willie said sheepishly, 'No kiddin', honest.'

'Now what do you think of that?' Harry Farthing broke off at this point to exclaim loudly. 'Ah! and here comes our third student. Now the trio is complete.'

As he took off his coat Roddy Canner stared at Harry Farthing. Roddy was a plump boy who had had glandular trouble and for years had suffered the jest of being Fattie. Now, with the help of drugs, the glandular disturbance was being arrested.

Of the three, Roddy had the least to say, perhaps because in any retaliation he knew he would suffer most. Harry Farthing knew this too, so Roddy was his main target. He said now, 'Coo! I bet you've been stuffing your kite over the weekend . . . What you put on, half-a-stone? It puzzles me, Canner, why you ever took on a job like this. You've got to be thin and wiry like our little darling here' – he nodded at Joe as he made a play with his name – 'because you never know but at any minute you're goin' to be pushed up a flue . . . What did YOU say?' He swung round towards Joe, then walked menacingly towards him. 'Go on, say it again.'

He now thrust his big face in front of Joe's. 'I dare you to say it again.'

Joe swallowed deeply; then jerking his chin, he said, 'All right then. I said, somebody should push *you* up a flue.'

As he finished speaking Joe sprang backwards and, grabbing a piece of wood from a bench, he

11

held it before him as he ground out, 'You touch me, Harry Farthing, and I'll give you this.'

Both Willie and Roddy were standing gaping, wide-eyed and open-mouthed, as Joe confronted the man who was, without exaggeration, twice the size in height and breadth of Joe, and their expressions said plainly that they thought he had gone stark staring mad.

Joe himself was thinking something along the same lines. Harry Farthing just had to grab him by the shoulders and he knew he would go flying through the air like the man on the Flying Trapeze. But Harry Farthing didn't grab him by the shoulders. What he did was laugh. It was a deep rusty chuckle at first, and then his head went back and he bellowed. He was bellowing when Mr Ripley came upon them.

'What's this?' said the ganger. 'What's up here?' Mr Ripley was a man of experience and he knew that Harry Farthing's laughter and young Joe standing at the ready with a stick in his hand didn't mean they'd been exchanging a joke. He looked from one to the other, then said, 'Come on, break it up. None of this here. As for you, Farthing, I'd pick one of me own size if I was you. It's nothing to your credit tacklin' little 'uns.'

'Who was tacklin' him?' said Harry Farthing, sulkily now.

'Well, it didn't look as if you were about to shake hands although you were laughing. Now, now.' Mr Ripley thrust his arm out as he added, 'I want to hear no more; there's work to be done. It's Monday mornin' an' let's start as we mean to go on. You, Styles, go up top with Farthing here; Bill Wheatley's up there, he's plenty for you to

12

do. Canner and you, Darlin', come along of me; we don't want you to go to school the morrow an' say you haven't learned anything, do we?' He pushed Joe playfully in the back, then added 'You can drop that stick; you don't need it any longer.'

And so Monday started. And it followed the usual pattern, and at times Joe was so busy that he forgot about home and what he was going back to tonight.

It was again dark when they came through the shipyard gates. They had been hurrying amidst a dense mass of men, but now the stream spread itself out, thinning in its progress along streets and roads.

Joe had little to say, leaving all the chatter to Willie, because his mind was again taken up with thoughts of his mam and dad. Willie, on the other hand, chatted incessantly; and now he demanded, 'Did you hear w . . . what I said, man?'

'No, what did you say?'

'You're miles away, you have been all day. I said, are you c . . . comin' to the club the night?'

'What, and stand watchin' you and them toeing the line?'

'I want to learn, man. And you should an' all.'

'If you were going to learn you would have done it afore this. When you get in the club what do you do? Stand like a stook. Wild horses wouldn't get you on the floor.'

'What about you? You won't go on either.'

'There's a difference; I've never wanted to dance, never.'

'Afraid of being trodden underfoot in the

13

rush?' Willie gave a side jump into the gutter as he made this quip, and Joe, looking at him disdainfully, said, 'There's big worms and little worms an' as I've said afore it's the big ones that get caught first 'cos they're always sticking their necks out.'

'Aw, I was only kiddin' you man ... By the way, I didn't say so afore but I thought you were a bit barmy to stand up to Harry Farthing like you did this mornin'; he'll have it in for you after this.'

Joe looked at his pal sideways and said with heavy sarcasm, 'Well, if I'd only been as big as you I wouldn't have dreamed of standin' up to him, but being my size I couldn't do anything else, could I?'

'Aw, man, go on.' Willie now pushed him, then said, apologetically, 'Well, you know me; I just don't like rows. I think if you can laugh things off it's best in the long run.'

Joe's scornful glance was lost on Willie in the dark, but when Willie said again to him, 'Well, are you coming to the club, I want to know?' Joe answered, 'Look, what about us going to the Tech Club. As I said on Saturday I'd like to take up boxing.'

'Aw, man, they're a snooty lot. I've told you.'

'What do you know about it, you've never been to try? Roddy goes. He plays badminton, and on Friday nights he goes to the chess club.'

'Ah, he's stuffy.'

'You're ignorant, that's what you are, Willie Styles, ignorant.'

'All right, I'm ignorant, so I'll remain ignorant. You go to the college club and get all high hat.'

'You don't know what you're talkin' about, man.' Joe shook his head slowly. 'All the societies are for us.'

'What! The fencing, an' the squash, an' the sub-aqua? An' the golf? Ah, don't be daft.'

'I'm not daft, it's you that's daft. The college sports and everything is for us students, it's in the book.'

'Well, you try goin'.'

'I will if you come with me; I don't want to go on my own.'

'Well, you'll just have to because I'm not going there. How many in the plumbing set go to the club?'

'Six of them to my knowledge. Two are in the sailing club, and you know those two from Redhead's yard, well, they're doing judo.'

'Nice for them.' Willie's tone was mimicking now and Joe said helplessly, 'Oh lor! I don't know why I put up with you.'

'Are you comin' along the night?' Willie persisted.

'No, I'm not.'

'Good,' said Willie; 'see you there.'

As he turned and hurried away up a side street Joe called after him. 'You'll be lucky.' Then thrusting his hands deep into his pockets, he walked on home, more slowly now; there was no need to hurry.

Other nights he hurried home so that if his mam hadn't got in he could set the table and have the kettle on before his dad arrived, but somehow he knew that tonight his grannie would have been down from her flat up above them and she'd have the tea ready for his dad. She always did this

15

after his mam and dad had a row and it made things worse.

And he was right. He smelt the tea as soon as he opened the door. She had been baking. He went through the kitchen and looked at the table all nicely set, and in the middle a big plate of freshly baked scones and another of tarts, and under the grill in the scullery a shepherd's pie was browning.

Sometimes he hated his grannie, yet there was a time when he had liked her; and she had always been nice to him; she still was, which made it worse.

He had just finished washing himself when his dad came in the back door, looked at him and said, 'Hello there', and Joe answered, 'Hello, Dad'. Then he watched him take off his coat, hang it on the back of the door and walk towards the kitchen. He didn't go in, he just looked round, then he came back to him and said, 'Your mother not in yet?'

Joe shook his head and watched his father bite on his lip. 'Have you seen your grannie?'

'No. I've only been in about ten minutes; she wasn't here when I came in.'

'But she's been in, hasn't she?' He looked towards the kitchen, then towards the stove, and added flatly, 'This'll help matters; this is sure to help matters.'

'Why don't you tell her, Dad?' asked Joe softly. 'I mean me grannie. Tell her to stop it.'

'Why should I? Now you tell me.' His father came towards him, and looked into his face and said again, 'Now you tell me why I should stop me mother coming down to make us a meal when me wife doesn't bother, eh?'

It was some seconds before Joe spoke, and then

he said, 'Mam would. She did it afore, she used to push it all in. An' if she didn't get home on time you got the tea yourself, you remember?'

Mr Darling straightened himself up and nodded his head, saying slowly, 'Yes, yes, I remember; but those days are gone, things have changed, people change. They do you know, Joe.' He jerked his head at him. 'Even the best. Something gets into them and they change. Well—' he went to the stove and lifted the pie from under the grill, saying, 'I don't see any reason to waste good food; it isn't that we get an overdose of it these days. Come on, lad, and have your tea.'

Joe was hungry but he found it difficult to eat. He was waiting for the sound of his mother's footsteps coming up the backyard, and when he did hear them he stopped eating and looked at his dad. But his dad went on eating, even with apparent relish now.

Joe watched his mam come from the scullery into the kitchen; he saw her look at the table, then at his dad, and when she said calmly, 'Very nice, very nice I'm sure', before going into the bedroom, he felt it wouldn't take much more to make him sick.

When after a while his mam didn't come into the kitchen he excused himself from the table and, going into his own room, he changed his clothes, then sat down on the edge of the bed and wondered what he would do with himself the night.

He should do more homework but he knew he couldn't put his mind to it, he had enough done to get by the morrow at school. He could go round to Willie's, then go to the club, but he felt he'd

17

had enough of Willie for one day too; as for going to the club, what would he do there? Play table tennis, or do as Willie did, stand and watch other people dancing? The other alternative was playing draughts or chess, or drinking pop and nattering. There was nothing in any part of this programme that appealed to him, it all seemed very boring, yet when his mam and dad were all right nothing seemed to bore him, he seemed to enjoy everything; aye, even watching other people dancing.

Mr Howard, who ran the club, used to say there was a mark around all dance floors. It was about three feet from the wall and once you stepped over it it was like jumping in off the deep end, you were never frightened any more. Aye well, he wasn't much of a swimmer if it came to that, for he had never jumped in from the deep end.

It was half an hour later when he decided there was nothing for it but to go round to Willie's. When he went into the kitchen again his mam was ironing. She smiled at him and spoke as if nothing was wrong. 'Going to the club?' she said, and he answered, 'Yes, for a little while'.

'Enjoy yourself,' she said, and he nodded at her, then he looked at his dad sitting by the fire, but his dad was reading the paper, or pretending to. His dad was a small man, dark and thin; he himself was small, dark and thin, but he still had time to grow bigger than his dad. It was his daily hope that he would. Not that he didn't think his dad was all right, he did, his dad was a good sort. And his mam was all right an' all. Oh aye, his mam was one of the best. Then how was it that his mam and dad went for each other like fighting cocks.

For weeks now they had been rowing. Looking

18

back, their fighting seemed to stretch down the years. It had an' all, because they had been at each other since his grannie came to live above them. That was nearly three years ago. Nothing had gone right since because she was always interfering, taking his dad's side against his mam; and his mam was high spirited and wouldn't stand for it.

His grannie had her own front door, and back door and her own rent book and she was always talking about being independent, which his mam said was a laugh.

As he went out he thought, wouldn't it be wonderful if when he came back they were laughing together, sitting at the table and eating and laughing together like he remembered them doing; but there wasn't much hope of that with his grannie upstairs, because even a laugh would bring her tearing down to find out what it was all about.

Joe now walked in the opposite direction to that which he took when he was going to work. Willie lived at the far side of the Chichester and the shortest way from Mabel Street to the Chichester was to cut through Bertram Street and across Dean Road. To do this he took some well-known short cuts. One was up an alley way and along by a row of warehouses known as Brick Fields Gate.

Years ago he used to come quite a lot to Brick Fields Gate. When he was short of a copper for the pictures he used to ask his mam for some old rags, and jam jars in particular, and take them along to the end of Brick Fields Gate where Mr Prodhurst, or Taggerine Ted, as he was known locally, had his yard.

Joe was actually thinking about Taggerine Ted

as he came to the end of the row of warehouses and to the double gates that led into Mr Prodhurst's scrapyard and it gave him a bit of a start when, in the lamplight, he saw a man standing there. At first he thought it was Mr Prodhurst, and then he thought it wasn't because he looked so old; and then when he spoke he knew it was.

'Hello, lad,' said Mr Prodhurst. 'Are you in a hurry?'

'No, not really,' said Joe. 'Did you want something?'

'I wonder, lad, if you'd run to the chemist for me and get me a bottle? It's me leg you see. It's given out, and the bottle's for me chest.' He coughed and the sound came as a deep, painful, jangling as if there were lots of things loose inside Mr Prodhurst. 'Will you do it for me?'

'Aye. What is it you want?'

'It's on this bit of paper. There's the money; it'll be three-and-sixpence.'

'I might have to wait,' said Joe; 'I'd go indoors if I were you. I'll fetch it in to you.'

'Will you, lad? That's kind of you. All right, I'll go on in. I'll leave the gate open. Just come through the yard; you'll see the light through the window.'

'All right,' said Joe. 'I won't be a tick.'

As he hurried towards the main road and the chemist he smiled to himself. It was funny that wasn't it, thinking about Mr Prodhurst at that minute and him standing at the door and asking him to go a message?

He was back within five minutes and when he pushed the gate open and went into the yard he thought, Eeh! it just looks like Steptoe's yard.

In the light from the window he picked his way around a jumble of old iron, then knocked at the door.

'Come in, come in,' Mr Prodhurst cried, and Joe went in, only to stop dead within the doorway. Eeh! as he said to himself later, he had never seen anything like it, even on the telly. Steptoe's room was a palace to this. There was no shade on the electric bulb and it showed up an old iron bed standing in one corner of the room, a square wooden table in the middle, a number of chairs, a chest of drawers and a conglomeration of boxes of all shapes and sizes lining the walls. It wasn't until he stood near the table and handed the old man his medicine and his change that he noticed that the boxes were full of books. The up-sided boxes held ordered rows of books, but the ones standing on their bottoms looked as if the books had just been thrown into them. Yet in spite of the jumble the place looked sort of bare, and clean.

'You ... you lookin' at my library?' Mr Prodhurst turned his unshaven face towards the wall behind him. 'I like books. Always read books. All my life I've read books. Do you read?'

'Well, some kinds of books, technical books,' said Joe.

'Oh, technical books.' Mr Prodhurst nodded at him. Then looking at the change in his hand, he picked out a sixpence and handed it to Joe, saying, 'Thanks, lad.'

'Aw, I don't want that.'

'Not enough?'

21

'Oh no!' Joe's voice was hard. 'It isn't that. I just don't want anything for running a message.'

'You don't?'

'No.'

'Well, well, that's a change. They'd take your hand off for it round here; can't get them to go for less than sixpence, not even for a loaf.'

'You're kiddin'.'

'No, I'm not kiddin'.' Mr Prodhurst's face was straight now. 'One time a bairn would go for all yer groceries and you'd give him a lump of sugar, but them days are gone. They ask what they're goin' to get afore they'll go.'

'You must ask the wrong ones,' said Joe smiling quietly.

'Aye, perhaps I do.' The old man now peered into Joe's face and after a moment he said, 'What's your name, lad?'

'Joe Darlin'.'

'Joe Darlin'. You'd be still at school I suppose?'

'No, I'm apprenticed in the shipyard, marine plumbing, an' I go to the Technical College, you know, twice a week.'

'You do?'

'Aye.'

'Eeh! that's grand. Look, would you like a sup of tea?'

'No thanks I've just had me tea.'

'Well, can you spare a minute? Would you like to sit down?'

Joe glanced round the room; then he sat down on a seat the old man indicated and, joining his hands between his knees, said on a laugh, 'I used to come to you years ago, Mr Prodhurst.'

'You did?'

22

'Aye, when I wanted coppers for the pictures I used to bring you rags.'

'It's a wonder I don't remember you; it's not often I forget faces.'

'Oh, it must be four or five years since, when I was about ten; I'm fifteen now.'

'Fifteen, are you? That's an age.' The old man jerked his head and Joe laughed. 'Do you know how old I am?'

'No,' said Joe.

'I'm seventy-eight, come December the twenty-fourth. I was born on a Christmas Eve. Nice time to be born on a Christmas Eve, don't you think?'

'Aye,' said Joe. 'You've been here a long time,' said Joe conversationally now. 'I mean, I remember you from when I was a little lad, and I remember me dad saying he knew you when he was a little lad.'

'I've been here all me life. Me mother ran the business after me dad died. I was only three months when me dad died and I was just on five when I started helping her. I used to sit up on the cart with her and she used to go round yelling, "Rags! bottles an' bones!" ' He imitated a high, almost unintelligible, call and Joe laughed outright.

'You live by yourself?' said Joe.

'No, not entirely, lad. I have The Gladiator. I'll never be alone as long as I've got him.'

'The ... the Gladiator?' Joe screwed up his face.

'Me horse.'

'Oh, your horse.' Joe's head was back, his mouth was wide and his eyes bright. 'I've never

23

heard a horse called The Gladiator. Gladiators were Romans.'

'Aye, they were that, lad, and they were called Gladiators because they were brave. And my horse is a brave horse, a fine horse, and so I named him The Gladiator. Listen, that's him. He knows I'm talkin' about him. Oh, he knows.'

There was a neighing sound from beyond the wall, and Joe looked towards the fireplace and the old man said, 'His stable's just t'other side. I don't need to go outside, I had a door put in from the room. Come and have a look.'

Joe got up and followed the old man. The process was very slow because Mr Prodhurst sort of dragged one leg after him.

They went through the door in the corner of the room and Mr Prodhurst switched the light on, and there, opposite to them, lying on a big pile of clean straw, was the oldest looking horse Joe had ever seen in his life.

'Aren't you going to get up and say hello?' Mr Prodhurst was talking as if to another person and the horse responded as if he was a person, for, struggling slowly to his feet, he stood up and came towards the old man and Joe.

The Gladiator was a big horse and Joe had the impression of bones sticking out of him at all angles from his body. When the animal put his head down to Joe and pushed him gently in the chest Joe almost fell over backwards, and not a little with fright.

'He likes you, he's taken to you; he doesn't do that with everybody. Oh yes, he likes you. He's choosey, is The Gladiator.'

24

Mr Prodhurst now moved towards the manger and, looking down at it, said, 'You didn't make much of your tea, did you?' Then turning to Joe he added, 'His appetite isn't what it used to be. He doesn't get much exercise now and when you don't get exercise your appetite's likely to suffer. Horses and men, we're all alike. I used to take him up on to the common every Sunday. Oh, he did enjoy that, he looked forward to it. But what with me leg and one thing and another it's been impossible lately. Still, he does well enough, don't you?'

The horse now placed his muzzle against the side of Mr Prodhurst's head and the way he moved it was for all the world, Joe thought, as if he were saying, 'Yes, I do well enough.'

'Go on, back to bed with you.'

Joe's eyes widened as the horse turned about, went to the corner and slowly lowered itself down on to the straw again.

When they were back in the room Mr Prodhurst said, 'There, what do you think of him?'

Joe daren't say what he thought, except that it was wonderful the way the horse knew what was being said to him.

'Are you in a hurry, lad?'

Joe hesitated before answering. Was he in a hurry? If he went to Willie's he would only go to the club. Somehow he thought it would be more fun talking to this old fellow than listening to Willie. He had got tired of Willie's nattering lately and, what was more, he sensed that Mr Prodhurst was sort of lonely, even in spite of having The Gladiator. Eeh! What a name to give a horse. And what a horse to have such a name.

The Gladiator. He thought now that if his mam and dad had been kind with each other he would have made them die laughing when he got home the night and described The Gladiator and all his bones.

He became aware that Mr Prodhurst was staring at him from under his shaggy brows and he said quickly, 'No, I'm in no hurry. I was just on me way to see a pal, but I work with him so I get enough of him.' He gave a little hic of a laugh and Mr Prodhurst said, 'One of those, eh? Is he a know-all?'

'Aye, a bit,' said Joe. 'He never stops talkin', but he's funny; he stammers, you see.'

'Stammers does he?' Mr Prodhurst now moved his head solemnly up and down. 'Well if he does that, lad, there's a reason for it. There's a reason for everything you know. I've read a little about what makes folks stammer and blush and such like. They're not sure of themselves. That's it, they're not sure of themselves.'

'Oh,' said Joe, 'is it?'

'Aye,' said Mr Prodhurst. 'Sit yourself down,' he said again, 'and tell me: do you like going to the Technical School? I've never been round that way for years but I understand it's a fine place now.'

'Yes, it is,' said Joe with a touch of pride in his voice; 'It's one of the best in the country. You can learn anything there, even to be a captain of a ship. And coo! you want to see the captains that are teachers. They're all in the prospectus. It's a big thick wad of a book.' He demonstrated. 'And the other teachers . . . they're all called lecturers you know.' He nodded towards the old man.

26

'There's hundreds of them, hundreds, I'm not jokin'.'

'You don't say.'

There was an impressive pause before Joe continued, 'They come from all over the place to the college. You know you're lucky to get in, they don't take everybody.'

'No?' said Mr Prodhurst.

'No,' said Joe. 'And you've got to mind your p's and q's lest you get the push.'

Mr Prodhurst now sat back in the chair and smiled gently before he said, 'You like being at the college then?'

'Oh aye.' Joe jerked his head. 'But in a way you know I wish I could have stayed on at school and got me "O" levels; them's the exams, you know.'

'Yes, yes, I know,' said Mr Prodhurst.

'Well, if I'd got them I might have been able to go full time to the college.'

'You would like to have gone full time?'

'Oh yes.' Joe shook his head slowly from side to side, then with wisdom garnered from three months in the adult world, he added, 'You know, you don't know what you want when you're at school. There are career masters who try to sort you out. Well, they do all right with them that's got brains, you know, got it up top—' he tapped his forehead – 'but for blokes like me, a bit slow off the mark like, well they don't bother much.'

'If you want my opinion,' said Mr Prodhurst quickly, 'I wouldn't say you were a lad that was slow off the mark.'

'No, no,' Joe now agreed with him, 'not in that way. No, nobody puts one over on me, an' I can stand up for meself, but I didn't sort of grasp

27

things very quickly at school and unless, well, unless you show some signs of being a flier you know you're lost in the crush, and yet ... Now this is what I can't understand.' He leant forward across the table towards Mr Prodhurst and he wagged his finger to emphasize his point. 'At the Tech I'm learnin' like a house on fire. Mr Guest, he's the one that takes us for the full day, he had me out to the board demonstrating because I'd answered his questions like that.' He snapped his fingers. 'It's funny, you know, but I just lap everything up there and it's not hard like. We get a lot of homework, and I don't mind doing it, but if anybody had mentioned homework when I was at school I would have passed out, and for two reasons, one because the master thought I was capable of doing it, and the other because I knew I wasn't.' He was leaning back in his chair now laughing loudly at his own joke, and Mr Prodhurst with him.

'Look, I'm going to make a cup of tea,' said Mr Prodhurst now; 'You'll drink it when it's put afore you, dry or not.' And on this the old man limped over to the stove and thrust the black kettle into the heart of the fire, and Joe sat back in his chair and thought, Funny how I can talk to him and him so old.

And Joe talked to Mr Prodhurst for the next two hours, and when he at last rose to take his leave the old man accompanied him to the door, and there he said, 'It's a long time since I enjoyed a crack like the night's, lad. Now I'm not going to press you, and I don't want you to put yourself out, but any night that you're passing the door's always open and you'll be welcome.'

'Oh thanks,' said Joe. 'Thanks. I'll look in on you again some time and perhaps get your medicine for you and—' he stretched his neck upwards – 'save you a tanner into the bargain.'

They parted on loud laughter and as Joe made his way home he couldn't help but smile to himself when he thought of all the places he could have spent the evening, including the Youth Club, the pictures, the Bowling Alley in Jarrow, and not forgetting any one of the clubs at the college, and he had to go and spend it in a ragman's room, and by! what a room. Yet he had enjoyed himself. And he had met The Gladiator. Oh aye. The Gladiator. By! he did wish he could tell his folks about The Gladiator, but as things stood they wouldn't see the funny side of it. . . .

When he entered the house he found his mother alone in the kitchen. She was standing with her hands on the mantelpiece looking down into the fire and she didn't turn towards him, not even when he said under his breath, 'Where's Dad? . . . In bed?'

She didn't answer for some seconds and then her reply came in the form of her indicating the ceiling with the lift of her head.

Joe stood by the table, his head bowed. That had really torn it. His dad hardly ever went upstairs. There was no need because his grannie was nearly always down here. She would come in and sit for hours and hardly open her mouth. It put a damper on any conversation.

'Joe.' His mother was facing him now, her eyes were all red with crying, her nose was red too, and her lips were trembling. 'Joe,' she said again.

'Aye. Mam, what is it?'

'Look! I'm going to ask you something and I want a straight answer. If your dad and me separate who do you want to live with?'

For the second time that evening he wanted to be sick. He felt his cheeks moving upwards, taking his lip with them. He screwed up his eyes and shook his head, and when his mother said again, 'Joe, I want an answer,' he looked her straight in the face and said, 'I don't know.'

'What!'

He realized that his answer had come as a shock to her.

'You mean you've got to think about it?'

'Yes, aye. Look, Mam. I've never thought about you separating. I . . . I want to live with you both, not one or the other.'

She had turned from him and was standing looking down into the fire again, and after a moment he walked slowly away and into his room and, throwing himself on the bed, dressed as he was, he punched his fist deep into the pillow as he repeated again and again, 'Oh Lord alive. Oh Lord alive.'

# Two

'Where you off to the night ... that old man's again? It isn't healthy; you'll be catching something. Bringing something home an' all, fleas or bugs.'

'I won't,' said Joe sullenly. 'I've told you afore, he's clean; even the stables where the horse is it's cleaner than some houses around here. I've told you.'

'You can't tell me an old man like that can keep himself clean with all those rags around him.'

'He hasn't taken in rags for years; it's all old iron. And he's stopped buying these last two years; he's just getting rid of what he's got.'

'Be that as it may—' Mrs Darling poked her face down to Joe's – 'it isn't healthy, I'm tellin' you. What does a lad like you want spending three nights a week alongside an old man for? Now Willie'll be around in a few minutes and you get yourself out with him. Anyway I thought you were going to join the boxing club at the college.'

'Mr Prodhurst is showing me how to box.'

'What! an old man of seventy-eight showing you how to box. Don't be silly, boy.'

'He is.' His attitude was defiant now and his voice loud. 'He's done boxing. He's showing me

31

how to use me feet like Cassius Clay; he says Cassius Clay boxes with his feet and . . .'

'Yes, yes, I know, he's the greatest. I've heard that before, it's got whiskers, but if you want to learn to box go to the right place.'

Joe drew in a deep breath, then attacked the remains of his tea. Lifting up the chop bone he began to gnaw at it until his mother, her voice like the crack of a whip, said, 'Stop that! Haven't I told you not to pick a bone up in your hand.'

'But I don't enjoy it any other way, Mam.'

'You've got a knife and fork there, haven't you?' She stabbed her index finger towards the table. 'Well use it. And don't eat like an animal.'

Eat like an animal? Eh! His mam had changed towards him lately. He could date it back to the night she had asked him to give her a straight answer as to whether he would like living with her or his dad. That was a month ago, and the situation in the house had, since then, become stationary in a way. But there was a fear growing in him lately that he would return one night from work and find his mother gone, and his grannie in charge, and he had asked himself the question what he would do if that happened. But he couldn't answer it, because he couldn't see himself saying to his dad, 'I'm going to live with me mam', because he liked his dad. But then he liked his mam an' all; and in an odd kind of way he liked his grannie, even though she was a mischief maker. But you couldn't really dislike anybody who had been kind to you for as long as you could remember, somebody who always had a bag of taffy kicking about when you went to see them, and would fork out picture money when you were broke. You couldn't really dislike anybody who had been as kind to you as that.

It was all very difficult and worrying; it was even interfering with his work. Mr Guest had had a word with him after the class had finished the other day. 'What's the matter, Joe?' he had said. 'Your work is not keeping up with the promise you showed at the beginning. Anything wrong?' To this he had answered, 'No, Sir.' And Mr Guest had looked at him for a long time before he said, 'A lot depends on what form you show here. You know that, don't you. You know a report is sent to the yard about you?'

He had merely nodded to this, and Mr Guest had said, 'You like coming to the college?' It was a question and Joe's head had come up immediately as he replied, 'Oh yes, Sir, I love it.'

'I thought you did,' said Mr Guest. 'And you say nothing is wrong.'

When Joe's gaze flicked to the side Mr Guest asked quietly. 'Is there trouble at home?'

Joe was on the point of denying this vehemently, but instead he swallowed and bowed his head, and Mr Guest said, 'Ah well, now we know where we are. But you mustn't let this get on top of you. People have to sort out their own lives; you've got your future to think about and quite a bit depends on how well you do in class. Now, you get back to where you were a few weeks ago and you have nothing to worry about.'

He had thanked the master and determined that that was what he was going to do. He was going to work like he had done when he first joined.

And the determination had stayed with him

33

until he had opened the door that evening, and there they were going at it hammer and tongs.

They gradually stopped when he stood looking at them, but the hour of silence that followed was, to Joe, as nerve racking as their fighting . . .

He was almost ready to leave the house when Willie came in. He knocked on the back door, opened it immediately, poked his head round and called, 'All r-right if I come in, Mrs Darling?'

'Yes, yes, of course, Willie.'

'Eeh! by, but it's cold; enough to freeze the hunkers off you . . . That's a grand fire.' After nodding towards the fireplace he turned his attention to Joe and said, 'Hello there, Joe.'

Joe looked at him but didn't answer. You'd think they hadn't met for a week and it was just over an hour and a half since they had parted.

'How's your mother?' asked Mrs Darling politely.

'Oh, she's fi . . . fine; she's in the middle of baking, making her Christmas p . . . puddin's. You know what, she says I can have a p . . . party at Christmas. Invite the lads, you know.'

'Oh, that'll be very nice,' said Mrs Darling.

At this point Mr Darling came out of the bedroom. He was dressed for outdoors, and he smiled at Willie and said, 'Hello there, lad,' and Willie said, 'Hello, Mr Darling.'

'So you're going to have a party?' said Mr Darling.

'Aye,' said Willie.

'Any chance of an invite?' said Mr Darling.

'Ho!' Willie laughed, 'It's just for the lads.'

'Aw, that's a pity.'

Joe looked at his father. He was acting as if

34

everything was normal in the house. He always did when anybody came in; and he always pulled Willie's leg. He thought Willie was a laugh, and he was if you didn't have too much of him.

His dad was now saying 'Well, if you won't invite me to your party, Willie, I'll have to find somebody to take pity on me because I might be at a loose end at Christmas.'

The remark was very meaningful to Joe but it just evoked laughter from Willie.

'Couldn't fancy you at a loose end, Mr Darling,' he said, and Mr Darling replied, 'Couldn't see meself at one time either, Willie. But these things happen. Well I'm off, so long. So long, Joe.'

'So long, Dad.'

His dad had neither looked nor spoken to his mother and she sat by the fire as if she hadn't noticed. Joe looked at her. She had a lost, a lone kind of look about her that started up a pain under his ribs. With a swift movement he unbuttoned his overcoat, saying, 'I've changed me mind. I'm not goin' out. You can stay if you like and have a game of cards.'

'Aw, man.' Willie's chin had dropped slightly. 'You promised you'd come to the club; you promised you'd have a go.'

'I promised nowt of the sort, an' if I was to go with you I wouldn't be havin' any goes, if you follow me.'

A fortnight earlier Willie had forced himself over the three foot line surrounding the wall of the dance floor, and since that time he could think or talk of nothing else.

'Look, if you want to make a fool of yourself

35

you go on and do it, but I'm not going to join you.'

'You promised, man.'

'I didn't; you tried to put the words in me mouth, but you said them. I said I might come to the club but I said nothing about dancin'. You've gone dancin' mad. What do you mean to do with it anyway? Join the Bolshoi Ballet?'

'Bolshoi? What's that?'

'Ah, forget it.'

'Oh aye! The Bolshoi, I know, the Russians. I saw them on telly. Well, I could do the hunker dance anytime, I used to do it when I was a kid. Like this.' He dropped on to his hunkers and kicked his feet out three times before falling over on to his back.

Joe, on the point of saying something scathing, glanced at his mother. Her shoulders were heaving. He bit on his lip, then allowed his laughter to escape. They were all laughing together now, and Willie, at least, was happy. He was always happy when he got people laughing.

When Joe said to him, 'You're barmy, lad. That's what you are, you're barmy,' he said. 'Aye, I know. I'm goin' to see if I can get it treated on the National Health.'

Again they were laughing, and now Mrs Darling was pushing them towards the kitchen door. 'Go on, get yourselves out. Go on this minute.'

As Joe went to close the back door after him he looked towards the lighted window and he saw his mother standing with her two hands covering her face, and he knew she wasn't laughing now.

*

36

The band was blaring out the latest Top Pop, and Joe stood leaning against a stanchion of the door looking towards the wreathing, wriggling mass of couples. His gaze returned again and centred on Willie. What did he look like! Eeh! if he could only see himself, he was like a great big loose-limbed puppet dangling from strings. The girl he was with wasn't half his size, he always picked little-'uns; made him feel important, he supposed. Aw, why did he keep picking on Willie? Willie was all right; it was himself that was all wrong. He couldn't get the picture of his mother out of his mind as she stood with her hands over her face; she'd likely be crying her heart out at this minute.

'You do this?' He turned his head sharply and looked at the girl confronting him, and he almost stammered as bad as Willie when he replied. 'N . . . no. I can't do it.'

'Well, you'll never learn standing there, will you?'

He stared at the girl. Eeh! she was a cheeky thing; she wasn't backward in coming forward. He squared his shoulders and jerked his neck upwards out of his collar and said coldly, 'It isn't my line. I'm going to have a game of table tennis.'

As he turned from her she said, 'Huh!' and he felt as if he had been pushed in the back.

He played table tennis for half an hour, after which he had a bottle of coke and ate two packets of crisps, and when he went along the corridor to the dance hall again Willie was still dancing. He signalled to him and Willie waved airily back, indicating that he should come on to the floor. Joe indicated that he was going home, but even this did not divert Willie from his dancing.

So Joe left the club. But he did not go straight home. He made a slight detour, which brought him to Brick Fields Gate and Mr Prodhurst. When he knocked on the door the old man called, 'Come in. Come in,' and when Joe entered he saw that Mr Prodhurst was in bed.

'You bad?' He was standing over him.

'Not really, lad. Just me leg playing me up, and me chest was a bit thick.'

'You've been taking your medicine?'

'Oh yes; I couldn't do without that.'

'Have you still got some?'

'Enough to do me until tomorrow. I wasn't expecting you the night but oh, I'm glad to see you. Oh aye, sit down.'

But Joe didn't sit down. 'You're not very warm in here,' he said. 'I'll make the fire up and get some coal in.'

'Thanks, lad, thanks.'

When Joe had finished his task he said, 'The Gladiator? Have you been able to see to him?'

'Oh yes, I managed that. But go on in and have a word with him, he gets a bit lonely you know. Sometimes I think about moving me bed in there.' He laughed his deep throaty, rattling laugh.

Joe opened the door and went into the stable. The Gladiator wasn't lying down tonight, he was standing, not a couple of yards from the communicating door. It was as if he had been aiming to come through into the other room.

'Hello there.' Joe had to be careful where he stood when talking to The Gladiator because, taken unawares, the animal's big head could

38

knock him on to his back. The Gladiator neighed and rubbed his muzzle against Joe in the same way as he did with Mr Prodhurst, and Joe reached up and stroked his neck and said, 'You eat your tea the night?' Then glancing at the manger he said, 'No, you didn't. You've got to eat you know; can't keep your strength up if you go off your feed. There now there now, stop it.' He gently pushed the tossing head from him. 'Go on and lie down. Go on now. Mr Prodhurst is all right.'

The horse stood still for a matter of seconds, then turning, he clop-clopped across the cobbled floor to his bed of straw, and there he stood for another few minutes before settling himself down.

Back in the room Joe said, 'You know, he takes notice of me, he knows what I say to him just as if you were talking to him.'

'Oh, I said from the first he had cottoned on to you. He's very wise is The Gladiator, very wise.'

'Have you had anything to eat the day?' asked Joe.

'Yes, yes,' said Mr Prodhurst. 'I opened a tin of stew at dinner-time and I've finished the broth I made on Saturday. I'll make some more the morrow.'

Joe sat down by the bed, and after staring at Mr Prodhurst, whose face underneath the bushy growth of hair, looked sort of yellowish to him, he said, 'Don't you think you should have somebody in to look after you?'

'No, no, lad, I'm all right. I can see to meself, and I don't want any woman nattering around me. Never could stand them. I've always seen to meself and I can manage. Don't you worry, lad.'

'Have you had the doctor?'

'Not for a time.'

'Don't you think you should get him?'

'I've been thinking about it, but this'll pass. I get days when I feel just lazy like. But don't talk about me. Tell me, what have you been doing with yourself over the past few days?'

'Oh, the usual.' And now Joe went on to explain the usual: the incidents that happened at work, both in the yard and at the college, and he finished up by telling him about Willie and the Bolshoi Ballet.

Mr Prodhurst had met Willie twice and so he could appreciate the joke, but all of a sudden he stopped laughing and, leaning towards Joe, he said, 'Anything wrong, lad?'

'No, no, Mr Prodhurst, I'm all right.'

'Oh aye, I know you're all right in health but I've had the idea you've had something on your mind lately. Have you? Would you like to tell me? It would be like sort of talking to yourself, it would go no further. I see no one.'

Joe stared at Mr Prodhurst for quite a while; then of a sudden he said, 'It's me folks, me mam and dad. They're going to separate.'

'Aw,' said Mr Prodhurst, 'I'm sorry. I'm sorry. Is it all settled?'

'No, no, but it's in the air.'

'Well, there's nothing you can do about it, lad. But try not to worry. And that's easier said than done. Married folks have got to sort out their own tangle. What's the trouble? Another woman?'

'Oh, no,' Joe shook his head. 'Nothing like that. It's me grannie.'

'Oh, your grannie. Where does she come in?'

'She lives upstairs; she's lived there since me grandad died, and things have never been the same since.'

'Mother-in-law trouble. The same old story . . . Have you decided who you're going to make your home with when they break up?'

Joe bowed his head before he said, 'That's the snag. I just can't. You see I like them both.'

There was silence between them for a time before Mr Prodhurst said, 'It's a pity I'm not a bit younger; you could have come and lived with me. I would have liked that fine.'

Joe stopped himself from laughing. The old man's face was serious. He was lying back on the pillow now, his eyes looking towards the smoke-blackened ceiling, and Joe looked round the room. Come and live here, in this dump? But the old man had meant it. It wasn't a dump to him, it was his home. He looked at him again and he thought. He looks bad. I'm going to miss him when he's gone. The thought came as a surprise to him for it seemed to foretell that Mr Prodhurst's days were numbered, and this brought a new sadness to him, a painful sadness, almost equalling the pain that centred around his mam and dad.

Life was all sadness he decided. Everybody seemed to have troubles. There was no fun, except for people like Willie. Oh aye, people like Willie saw the funny side of everything.

# Three

It was a Friday and a week before Christmas and one of those days when irritations, injustices and bullying, mounting one on top of the other, caused Joe to tell himself that if tomorrow weren't Saturday he would run amuck with a three pound hammer in his hand. He was saying as much to Roddy Canner when Mr Ripley, putting his head round an aperture that would later become a doorway, shouted, 'You there, Joe, go along to the shop and get a dozen lengths of half-inch copper tubing, then take them up to D section. Have them signed for; here's the chit . . . Take Canner with you.'

Joe caught the slip of paper, looked at it; then making sure that Mr Ripley had gone, he said, 'Twelve lengths of piping; it's like being sent for a ha'porth of tar in a hundredweight drum.'

'It's likely because it's last thing in the week,' said Roddy. 'They won't draw anymore to have them lying around. You remember a while back when all that lead was nicked; copper piping is nearly as valuable the day.'

'Aye, I suppose you're right. Come on.' Joe clambered over the network of girders, then up on to the deck and to the stores.

It was fifteen minutes later when they returned carrying the pipes between them, and when they reached D section they were confronted, not by Alf Hoggarth who was in charge up here, but by their joint enemy, Harry Farthing. They had no sooner put in an appearance than he barked at them, 'It's comin' to something when it takes two of you to carry a few pipes. But of course I'm forgettin', one of you's so little he can hardly carry his breath. That's so, isn't it? Eeh!' He leered at Joe; then turning his attention to Roddy, he added, 'And the other's so fat and lazy, the only thing he can carry is his grub.'

The two boys stared at the big fellow. Then Roddy, turning about, said under his breath, 'Come on.' But Joe didn't come on. This was the last straw. Moreover, he had to get the pipes signed for. He stared angrily up at Harry Farthing. Then grabbing the paper from his pocket he thrust it at him, saying, 'Sign for them.'

'Sign for what?'

Joe tossed his head from side to side and answered cockily, 'One of us is too little and the other is too fat to do any work, but we're not dim like some folks I could mention. What do you think you've got to sign for? The pipes of course.'

As he jerked his finger down towards the pipes Harry Farthing came so close to him that Joe could see nothing but the top button of the man's waistcoat.

'You'd better mind who you're talkin' to, young 'un, because I could take you by the scruff of your neck and knock your brains out against the bulkhead, an' I will an' all if I have any more of it.'

Joe had to step back before he could speak, 'Well go on. Try it on,' he cried angrily. At the moment he was past fear, he was so fed up with everyone and everything that he didn't care what happened to him.

Harry Farthing stared down at him in amazement, then, the expression on his face altering, it showed what could have been begrudging admiration.

Again Joe wagged the paper in front of him. 'Are you goin' to sign it?'

'No, I'm not.'

'Well, you're not goin' to get the pipes; I'm taking them back.'

'You leave them where they are.'

Joe watched Harry's fists doubling themselves. He knew what he had said was true, that he could knock his brains out with one blow, but still he persisted. 'Mr Ripley said they had to be signed for and if you don't do it then I'll get somebody else.'

He looked about him. There was no one in sight on the section at the moment. Then of a sudden he felt his feet leaving the ground as Harry Farthing gathered a handful of his coat into his fist. And now Harry's words were almost spitting on to his face. 'You go back and tell Mr Ripley you left them with me an' it'll be all right.'

As Joe stared into the eyes looking into his it was as if a door was opening in his mind, and looking through it he saw again a number of incidents that had puzzled him over the last few weeks, and all concerning Harry Farthing. For instance, him staying last on a Friday night, not going for his pay until everybody else had gone, buying raffle tickets and not putting his name on the counterfoils, saying. 'Aw, it doesn't matter, I won't win anyway.' Then seeing Mr Ripley writing Harry Farthing's name in the margin from where the tickets had been torn; and that day when he found him sitting by himself at bait time reading a comic. But that was it, he hadn't been reading that comic, he had just been looking at the pictures.

Harry Farthing couldn't read or write.

He didn't mean to say it aloud but it came out on a whisper, 'You can't read or write.'

He thought for a moment that Harry was going to choke him and he gulped quickly, 'Well, that's nothin', man, it's nothin'; me dad's not very good at it either.' He didn't know how he thought up this lie so quickly.

The pressure on his clothes slackened and his toes touched the floor, but Harry still had hold of him. They were still staring at each other when Joe said quietly, 'Don't worry, I won't let on. But mind—' he wriggled himself free from the slackened grasp – 'it's not because I'm frightened of you. You know that, don't you? I'm not frightened of you, as big as you are.'

Again they were staring at each other, and then Joe, looking downwards, said, 'It's nothin' to be ashamed of, man. I was slow at school myself.'

Joe now picked up the piece of paper from the floor and, bringing a stump of pencil from his pocket, he wrote across the bottom 'Harry Farthing', and looking up at the big, silent fellow he said, 'There, it's done; there's nowt to worry about.'

Harry Farthing said nothing to this but, stooping and gathering up the pipes, he walked away, and after a moment Joe, too, walked away in the opposite direction.

All the pressure, irritation and anger, all the indignation of being the recipient of injustice was gone from him, and he thought, with a feeling that he didn't recognize as compassion, A big fellow like him and can't read or write; and there came to him Mr Prodhurst's saying: There was a reason behind everything, like Willie's stammering was the result of inner fear; and he understood now that Harry Farthing's inability to read or write was the reason behind his bullying.

Mr Ripley was at a bench looking at a diagram of inter-locking pipes when Joe handed him the receipt. 'Mr Hoggarth wasn't about,' he said; 'but Harry Farthing signed it.'

If Joe had sworn at him Mr Ripley couldn't have turned on him quicker. 'What did you say?' he said.

'I said Harry Farthing signed it.'

Mr Ripley looked at the chit, then looked at Joe. 'Who did you say signed it?'

Joe stared at Mr Ripley.

'Why did you sign this? . . . Come on, tell me. Why did you sign this?'

'Just because I did, I couldn't find him.'

Again Mr Ripley stared at Joe, and his voice very low now in order that it wouldn't carry to the other men at the end of the shop, he said, 'Harry Farthing's very touchy about this; 'tisn't everybody that knows, and them that does keeps their mouths shut. He could be a dangerous customer to come up against could Harry. Who told you?'

'Nobody, Mr Ripley. I asked him to sign it. I said if he didn't sign it I'd go and ask somebody else, and he grabbed me. And then I sort of knew; put two and two together so to speak.'

'And you told him?'

'Aye.'

Mr Ripley wetted his lips, then said, 'What did you do next?'

'Nowt. I told him it was all right. I said me dad was troubled that way an' all, although that was a lie. Me dad has a very good hand; he has to at his job – storekeeper.'

Mr Ripley doubled his fist and pushed it slowly against the side of Joe's head, and he smiled wryly as he remarked, 'You'll do, young 'un. And you know, somehow I don't think you'll have any more trouble with Harry Farthing. He can be a good friend can Harry, but a damn bad enemy. I know he's a bully but he's not to blame, he's had a rough deal. He's been pushed into more homes than a cat's got lives. Go on now, get on with your work and keep your mouth shut. Don't pass it on; if the other lads find out well and good, but what they don't know won't do them any harm.'

'Yes, Mr Ripley.' Joe went back to his work. He had an odd feeling about him, a sort of lucky feeling, as if he should be glad he was alive in spite of being only four foot eleven and a half inches.

The night before Christmas Eve Mrs Darling placed into a box a basin holding a Christmas pudding, a fruit cake with a paper frill around it, on top of which she put a piece of cardboard, and counted on to it a dozen mince pies.

'There, that should see him all right.'

'Thanks, Mam.' Joe smiled at her. 'It's good of you. I'll pay you for them.'

'Have I asked you to?'

'No, but there's a lot of stuff here and I know it costs money.'

'Hold your tongue ... What are you getting him?'

'A bottle of wine. I've got it, it's in the room. I paid nine and sixpence for it. It's a good one. And a pair of socks. It was no use getting him slippers; he shuffles round in his stockinged feet.'

'Eeh! he must be in a mess from what you tell me. I know I should look in and see him but very likely if I did I wouldn't let you go back there. In fact, I feel sure I wouldn't.'

'He's a nice old man, Mam.' Joe's face was straight. 'He's a good man, wise like.'

'Be that as it may, living with a horse!'

'He doesn't actually live with the horse, just next door.'

'From what you tell me he should be in a home.'

'Likely he would be if it wasn't for The Gladiator.'

'The Gladiator! Did you ever hear of such a daft name to give an animal.'

'I thought that an' all when I first heard it, Mam, but you get used to it, and when you know him it sort of fits him.'

'Well, there you are. Get yourself away. Oh, an' here's a carrot for The Gladiator.' She thrust the carrot at him and Joe put it in his pocket with a laugh. Then, his hand on the parcel, he asked quietly as he jerked his head upwards, 'What's she doing at Christmas?'

'Don't ask me, I don't know.'

'Is she coming down to dinner?' She turned her head over her shoulder and looked at him.

'It'll be a nice Christmas dinner if she does, won't it?' 'It won't be very cheerful even as things are.'

He now asked the question he had wanted to ask for days. 'How are things, Mam?'

She walked from him and into the scullery and came back with a tray of crockery in her hand before she said, 'It's difficult to answer at the moment.' She now put the tray down on the table and, still holding it, she looked down at it as she added, 'Your dad is up to something. I don't know what, it's just a feeling, but he's up to something.'

'He hasn't been going upstairs lately, has he?'

'No, but there's something, and I can't lay me finger on it. Anyhow you go on and get your presents to the old man. And don't worry. And mind how you go; it's like a skating rink outside.'

And it was like a skating rink outside. Joe almost lost his balance as soon as he put his foot on the pavement. It had been bad enough when he came home from work but now it was freezing even harder. It was no use trying to get a bus to Brick Fields Gate, it was much quicker to take the short cuts; but even so it was almost half an hour later when he pushed Mr Prodhurst's gate open, and then came to a standstill. The yard was as black as pitch. There was no light shining from the kitchen window, but there was a noise coming from the stable. It was The Gladiator, and the sound he was making was not really like a neigh at all, it was as if he was in pain or something.

Joe picked his way across the yard and

knocked on the door. Mr Prodhurst had likely fallen asleep and forgotten to put the light on, but it was nearly seven o'clock and he would have needed the light from four o'clock, because the whole day had been overcast with it snowing.

'Mr Prodhurst!' He called out the old man's name as he pushed the door open. Groping his way to the table he dropped the cardboard box and shopping bag on to it, then made towards the wall where the electric switch was.

When the naked bulb lighted the room he stood staring towards the bed. Mr Prodhurst was lying on the top of it fully clothed. His hands were joined together and resting on his stomach; his face looked very still; all of him looked very still. Joe couldn't make his legs move towards the bed; he had the desire to turn and run out into the yard, and into the street, anywhere but stay here.

'Mr Prodhurst!' The name was just a whisper now. 'Mr Prodhurst!' He again whispered the name as he moved across the room, and then he was standing looking down on the old man. Mr Prodhurst's eyes were closed and he looked as if he were asleep but Joe knew he wasn't asleep. He stood staring at him. He didn't look frightening, only very, very quiet, sort of relaxed looking.

He gave a great start when a loud neigh came from the next room. He turned towards the door. Poor Gladiator. Aw, poor Gladiator. And poor Mr Prodhurst. He had brought him all these things an' all. All day he had been thinking what he would say when he gave him the cake and things, all home-made. He jammed his teeth tightly down into his lower lip and screwed up his eyes, then went blindly into the stable.

The Gladiator was usually lying, or standing, in his stall but tonight he wasn't more than a yard from the door and at sight of Joe he made that strange sound again, a sound that wasn't horse-like at all, and Joe, going to him and resting his head against him, said, 'Poor fellow. Poor fellow.'

The horse, after tossing his head twice, became quiet, and Joe's voice cracked as he murmured, 'Come on, lie down, lad. Come on, lie down.' Turning the horse about he led him into the stall and, stroking his nose, he said softly, 'You know, don't you? You know.' And the horse remained still, almost as still as Mr Prodhurst.

Joe now looked at the manger. There was no seed hay in it tonight. He said brokenly, 'Stay put. I'll be back and get you something, but . . . but I must go and fetch somebody first.'

When he went into the kitchen again he didn't look towards the bed but made straight for the door, and closing it after him he ran slipping and sliding across the yard and into the road. Looking first one way and then the other he asked himself would he go home and get his mam or fetch the polis?

But the decision seemed to be taken out of his hands for when he reached the corner of the street a patrol car was turning in slowly from the main road, likely on its round of the warehouses, and he found himself shouting at it, 'Hie! Hie! Polis!'

The car drew up alongside the kerb and he bent down to the window and gasped, 'Will you come? There's an old man, Mr Prodhurst. I go and see him now and again. I . . . I think he's dead.'

The police looked at him for a moment, then said, 'Whereabouts, sonny?'

51

'Along at the end here, the Taggerine yard.'

'You mean Taggerine Ted?' said the other policeman.

'Aye, that's him.'

'Get in,' said the policeman, opening the back door of the car; and Joe got in, but within seconds he was out again and leading the way across the yard and into the room.

The two policemen stood looking down at Mr Prodhurst. Then they looked about the room; then they looked at Joe, and one of them said, 'When did you find him?'

'Not five minutes ago. Well, perhaps ten.'

When the neighing sound came from the other side of the wall the policeman turned in the direction of the stable and Joe said, 'That's his horse; he knows something's wrong.'

The two policemen looked at one another and then one of them said, 'I'll phone for the ambulance,' and went out.

'It was his birthday the morrow,' said Joe; 'I brought him a cake and things; me mother made them.' He looked towards the box and shopping bag on the table, and the policeman nodded understandingly, then said, 'He hadn't many friends, he was a bit of a recluse. He worked hard and he never did anyone any harm that I know of and yet he had to live like this, in this pig-sty.'

'He was happy,' said Joe; 'he had The Gladiator.'

'The what?'

'The . . . the horse.' Joe thumbed towards the wall.

'He called it The Gladiator?'

'Yes.'

52

The policeman smiled tolerantly and Joe felt he should defend Mr Prodhurst's right to call the horse The Gladiator if he wanted to, but policemen were policemen and you had to be careful what you said.

Joe was a bit hazy about the sequence of events in the next two hours. He knew the ambulance came in no time and he knew that he couldn't watch them put Mr Prodhurst on to the stretcher but went into the stable with The Gladiator, who was making that weird noise every now and again. But he couldn't remember if he quieted The Gladiator or if it was Mr Billings, the vet.

Mr Billings had come into the stable and spoken to the horse as if he knew him. 'I'm the vet,' he said; 'and you must be Joe. The old man mentioned you.'

'Aye,' said Joe. He was sitting on the straw near The Gladiator's head, because the horse seemed to like to have him there. 'What are you going to do with him?' he asked.

'There's only one thing,' said Mr Billings gently. 'He's a very old horse and they'll be together. He wouldn't want to be separated from the old man.'

Joe stared up at Mr Billings. 'How do you do it?' he said.

Mr Billings swallowed, moved his feet in the straw, then said, 'Oh, it's done very humanely, very humanely.'

Aye, thought Joe. Then he'd be boiled down and made into dog food. The thought drove him to his feet. 'Couldn't he be buried?' he said.

'No, no, they don't bury horses, not like that. Now don't worry. Has he had anything to eat?'

'I've given him his feed but he won't touch it.'

'I'd go home now,' said Mr Billings. 'He'll be all right.'

'He'll not,' said Joe under his breath.

'Well we can't do anything about it, can we?'

Mr Billings and Joe exchanged glances, and Joe, walking towards the door without looking at The Gladiator again, said, 'What time will you be coming the morrow?'

'Oh, I'll have to make arrangements, and it being Christmas Eve things will be difficult. I couldn't give you a definite time.'

'I'll come round first thing,' said Joe, 'and see to him.'

'That's kind of you,' said Mr Billings; 'but I could get in touch with the R.S.P.C.A. . . .'

'No,' said Joe quickly, 'I'll see to him.'

'As you wish. As you wish,' said Mr Billings soothingly.

Joe slowly gathered the box and the shopping bag from the table and as they went out of the door he said, 'What about locking up?' and Mr Billings answered 'Oh, I suppose the police will see to that. Anyway,' he added sadly, 'there's nothing to steal. He had nothing of any value to my knowledge. But' – he inclined his head – 'he always paid on the dot and never asked for charity. If he thought anything was wrong with the animal he called me in right away.'

They stood outside the main gate for a moment, then Mr Billings said, 'Good night and don't worry,' and Joe turned away without making any remark at all. And he didn't notice his feet slipping and sliding on the ice-covered streets; he had his chin buried deep in his collar, almost resting on the box, and his eyes cast downwards. He was glad it was dark. He hoped there was nobody at home when he got in because he wouldn't be able to talk about it without blubbering right out.

# *Four*

When Joe entered the kitchen at quarter past seven the next morning he was surprised to see his mother up and dressed and the table laid for breakfast. She turned to him and said, 'I didn't hear you stirring else I would have brought you a cup of tea in.' To this he just jerked his head because he was finding he couldn't talk properly, in fact he felt worse than he had done last night when he came home and found them both in the house and tried to tell them what had happened.

When his mother put a plate of bacon and eggs before him he looked at it, then without looking at her he pushed it to one side, mumbling, 'I couldn't. I just want a cup of tea.'

She leant towards him now and said softly, 'It's no good you know, Joe, getting upset like this; he won't know anything about it. Your dad says they do it very quickly . . . in the head.' She pointed to her temple and Joe screwed up his eyes and, tossing his head, in almost the same manner as The Gladiator himself did, cried out, 'Don't, don't, Mam! Haven't you any sense?'

His mother didn't reprimand him for this, but, her voice still quiet, she said, 'I'm sorry.' Then after a moment she added, 'But if you take my advice you won't go round there any more.'

'I'm going.' He was spooning sugar into his tea, two, three, four spoonfuls; then he stopped abruptly and looked down into the cup, and his mother took it from him, saying, 'Don't worry, I'll give you another.' And when she handed him a fresh cup he said to her, 'He's got to be cleaned out and have something to eat.'

He raised his head now to see his father standing in the doorway looking at him, and he thought, If he says, 'The condemned ate a hearty breakfast' I'll throw tea at him, straight I will, because his dad had the knack of capping things.

But Mr Darling didn't joke in an effort to ease the situation; instead, he said, 'Would you like me to come along with you?'

Joe stared at his father for a moment; then said, 'No. Thanks all the same.'

'It'll be no trouble; it's on my way to work.'

Joe shook his head and his father said no more.

When he was ready to go his mother came to the front door with him and as he stepped out into the bleak, breath-cutting morning she put her hand gently on his shoulder and whispered, 'It'll pass. I mean how you're feeling.'

Aye, they said everything passed, Joe thought as he walked down the street, but before it passed it had to be present, hadn't it? It was like being nearly round the bend with toothache and some bloke saying to you, 'I know how you feel, lad.' They didn't know how you felt, they only thought they did. If they knew how you felt they'd be crying out inside, 'I can't bear it', like you were.

And he was crying out inside now, 'I can't bear it. I can't bear it.' Yet at the same time he tried to take an objective view of the situation, telling himself that if anybody had told him three months ago that he'd be upset beyond measure about an old ragman dying, and at the thought of an old horse, who was ready to die anyway, being put to sleep, he would have said they were barmy. Yet here he was experiencing an anguish that no words in his vocabulary could explain.

When he opened the gate there was no sound, nor when he crossed the yard, and when he reached the stable door he couldn't open it because he was seized with a feeling of panic.

Mr Billings had been and taken him already.

When he thrust the door open and saw The Gladiator standing in his stall in that queer still way, he drew in a deep breath and, going towards him, touched the animal's muzzle and said softly, 'Hello there, boy.'

The Gladiator did not toss his head this morning; it was as if he knew the time for greetings was almost past, there was nothing more to look forward to, not even on the narrow horizon of the stable and the yard outside in which Mr Prodhurst had been wont to exercise him, and for which purpose he had made a circular path around the junk.

The Gladiator's attitude made Joe feel even worse, if that were possible, and he started to busy himself cleaning out the soiled straw and carrying it to a place near the main gate where

Mr Prodhurst stored it, and from where it was collected by a market gardener from the outskirts of the town.

He hesitated before taking fresh straw from the bale in the corner and putting it in the stall. But why not? For the time left to him, why not give him comfort, put all the straw down? On this thought he went back to the bale and tore out armful after armful of straw and heaped it on the floor beside The Gladiator. 'There you are, boy. There you are. Look, a nice bed,' he said gently. 'And, eat your breakfast.' He pointed to the manger.

The horse now jerked its head and nuzzled Joe's shoulder as if to say, Thank you. The affectionate gesture was too much for Joe, and he had to go into the other room. He had never seen it in the daylight before. Without the comforting glow from the fire, it looked terrible, and it smelt damp.

When The Gladiator began to neigh loudly, as he had done last night Joe, returning to the stable, stood looking helplessly at him from the doorway. He watched him toss his head wildly now, and he thought, He knows. He knows what's coming. Oh God! I can't stay in here with him. I just can't. It's like being in a cell with a condemned human, but I can't leave him alone waiting.

He looked at his watch. It was just turned nine o'clock. How long would he have to wait? It was freezing cold. He began to move about in a desperate effort to keep himself warm. Presently he came to a halt in front of the grime-stained window and through it he saw to his amazement

59

his mother coming up the yard, followed by a policeman. He met them at the door and his mother said, 'It's all right, it's all right. It was just that there's a letter for you and I thought I would come along . . .' Her voice trailed away.

The policeman smiled down on Joe. He was a new one, Joe noticed, but he seemed to know all about the situation for, holding out a letter, he said, 'This was found among the old man's belongings. It's addressed to you.'

Joe looked at the envelope and read, 'To Mr Joe Darling, Junior.' Then he looked at his mother and she said, 'Go on, open it.'

Slowly he slit open the envelope and drew out a folded sheet, in between which reposed a number of pound notes. He cast a quick glance at his mother again, and then at the policeman, before reading the letter. It said simply, 'Dear Joe, I'll be pushing up the daisies, at any rate nearer to doing it than I've ever been before, when you read this. You're a good lad, Joe. I've found that out over the past weeks. You've given me something to look forward to in my last days. You'll never really know what you did for me dropping in like that that night, or what your company has meant to me, so in return I'm leaving you The Gladiator. I enclose six pounds. That'll help you with his feed for a time, and you might get a little for the books. You're a bright lad, Joe, and you'll work out a way to keep him until his time comes, I'm sure of that. Just remember this, Joe. No kindness ever goes unrewarded. Your dear friend, Edward Prodhurst.'

Joe looked from his mother to the policeman

and back to his mother again. Then handing her the letter, he exclaimed on a high note, 'He's left me The Gladiator!'

'WHAT!'

'There!' He stabbed at the letter. 'He says I'm to have him and this money's to help keep him.'

While his mother was reading the letter he glanced back towards the stable. He wanted to rush to The Gladiator and shout, 'You're all right, lad, you're all right.' Then even before his mother, or the policeman, who was also reading the letter over her shoulder, could voice any comment, good, bad, or indifferent, he put his hand tightly over his cheek and groaned aloud, 'But ... but I can't. I can't see to him, I'll be at work.'

'Of course you will.' Mrs Darling's voice sounded full of indignation. 'It's an imposition. He should never have done such a thing. And six pounds! What's six pounds. There'll likely be rent to pay for this place ... Really! I never heard anything like it.'

The policeman looked sadly down at Joe and said, 'He was an old man and couldn't have understood things clearly; they get a bit like that as they get on. I understood the horse was to be put down the day. I think that's the best thing that could happen to it.'

'No! No!' Before Joe could go on his mother put in quickly, 'Well now, make up your mind. First you say you can't look after him and now you say you don't want him put down. But what am I saying? There's no need to make up your mind, you can't keep a horse. Where is it?'

Joe jerked his head, and Mrs Darling marched

into the stable, and there she let out a high, squeaking sound, and the policeman who was behind her, also gave vent to his feelings. But his was a deep chuckle, almost a laugh.

'Oh, my goodness! Did you ever see anything like it?' Her words were spaced as she addressed the policeman, and he said, 'No, I don't think I ever have. I saw it some years ago when it was pulling the cart, but it has deteriorated a lot since then. My! my!'

'That's settled it.' Mrs Darling marched out into the yard again, saying over her shoulder, 'You're letting them take it the day. Now say no more.'

'THEY'RE NOT GOING TO TAKE IT!'

Joe was standing inside the stable door.

'What!' She turned abruptly and confronted him.

'They're not going to take it. I'll ... I'll look after him somehow.'

'Don't be stupid, boy.'

'I'M NOT STUPID, MAM.' He was shouting again. 'I can get up an hour earlier in the mornings and I can pop back in my dinner break, and then I can see to him properly at night. He never got out much before; it won't make much difference now. Only he's not going to the knacker's yard.' His voice ended on an even louder shout, and she shouted back at him, 'Don't you talk like that to me. I'll let your dad deal with you.'

'I don't care who you get to deal with me, Mam, I'm not lettin' them take him. Look.' He grabbed at the letter she was still holding and, waving it almost in her face, he said, 'He's mine.

Legally he's mine. Mr Prodhurst has written it there in black and white.'

'Yes, he left it in black and white. He knew what he was doing, and he left you six pounds, didn't he? Six pounds! Well, just work out how much it takes to keep a horse, an' see how many weeks he'll last.'

'I'll deal with that when the times comes, Mam.'

'You'll have to. You'll have to.' She now marched out of the yard, leaving Joe and the policeman looking after her. Then the policeman, turning to Joe, said, 'She's right, you know.'

Joe answered nothing for the moment, but when he did he said stubbornly, 'I'm keeping him.'

'Well, I admire you anyway for having a try,' the policeman now said, and added, 'You'd better let them know; it'll save them coming with the van.'

'I don't know who they are,' said Joe. 'Mr Billings, the vet, he was seeing to it.'

'Well, you'd better get in touch with him, hadn't you?' The policeman now moved slowly away. Then turning and glancing at Joe over his shoulder, he added finally, 'Good luck, lad.'

Joe made no reply. Good luck. He'd need a lot of luck. By! Aye, he'd need a lot of luck.

He went into the stable now and, closing the door behind him, he stood looking towards The Gladiator. He was his. He might look like nothing on earth in horse flesh but nevertheless he belonged to him now. And it was a funny thing, when you got to know him you didn't think of him as odd or funny looking; it was only the first

63

sight of him that surprised you. The more you were with him the more you got the idea that he was an exceptional kind of horse.

He went slowly towards The Gladiator and, putting his arms around the big head, he pulled it to him and laid his face for a moment against its cheek, whispering as he did so, 'It's all right. It's all right. They're not going to have you.' Then abruptly he turned away and went into the other room. He found a cabbage, from which he tore off the outer leaves; picked up a carrot from a box; returned to the stable again and tried to tempt the horse to eat. But nothing he did or said would make The Gladiator nibble at his favourite tidbits. So, laying them near the edge of the straw, he said, 'Lie down. Go on, lie down. I'll be back, I won't be long. I've got to go and see Mr Billings and put things right. Go on now, lie down.'

In the room again he stood looking around him for a moment. He had an odd feeling, as if a great sorrow had been lifted from his heart yet at the same time a heavy weight had been placed on his shoulders. He actually straightened his back as if against the pressure; then shaking his head, he said aloud, 'Come on, get on with it.'

But there was one thing he must do before he left the place; lock up well, just in case they came and took him. He had seen some locks and chains in a box under the sink, and now he sorted out keys to fit the locks. This done, he bolted the horse door on the inside and went through the stables and locked the stable door on the outside; then taking a length of chain and a padlock he locked the outer gates.

64

Now, taking to the road because it had been sanded – and oblivious of the traffic – he ran all the way to Westhoe. He knew the number of Mr Billings's house because he had found a receipt for a visit in the cupboard.

When he rang the bell the door was answered by a girl of about fourteen. She had long black hair which fell down over her shoulders; it was tied at each side with a piece of ribbon just below her chin. She had round dark eyes and a plump round face and Joe's instant reaction at the sight of her was to think, 'Coo! she's a plain-un.'

'Could I see Mr Billings, please?'

'He's busy, and so's Mr Harding; they are operating on a dog.' She had a nice voice.

'Oh!'

'Did you want him to call?'

'No, no; I want to see him.'

'But I've told you, they may be half an hour or more yet, they're trying to save his leg. It was run over.'

He made a motion with his head that expressed sympathy, then said, 'Could I wait?'

'Well, he doesn't take surgery on a Saturday morning. Is it important?'

'Aye, it is.'

'About a dog?' She had her head on one side.

'No, a horse.'

'Oh, The Gladiator!' Her face had sprung into a wide smile and he found himself smiling back as he said, 'You know him?'

'Yes, Mr Prodhurst's horse.'

He looked at her for a moment, his face straight as he asked, 'You knew he was going to be put down the day?'

65

'Put down? The Gladiator? Oh no; Father didn't say.' She turned and looked into the hall towards a door at the far end; then looking at Joe again, her face twisted with concern, she said, 'Oh, poor thing.'

'Oh, not now. I mean he's not going to be put down now. That's what I've come to see Mr Billings about. Mr Prodhurst left a letter. The polis brought it round. He's left me The Gladiator.' He watched her face slide into another wide beam and when she said, 'Oh, that's marvellous,' he thought to himself, Well, I'm glad somebody thinks so besides me. She was all right, the girl, sort of nice.

'Come in,' she said. 'This is the waiting room.'

She showed him into a room off the hall that had a strong animal flavour about it; then she said, 'What's your name?'

'Joe Darling.' He thought she was asking because she wanted to put it down in an appointment book or something, but now she said, 'Mine's Anna Billings.'

'Oh!' He jerked his chin, then nodded his head.

After a moment she said, 'I'll come back and tell you as soon as they've finished.'

'Ta. Thanks.'

When the door closed on her he sat down, and in the quietness of the room he tried to form a plan whereby he could work eight hours a day, get his homework done at night, and see to The Gladiator in between times.

The enormity of the task was confronting him squarely when the door opened again and the girl came in, followed by a woman. She looked a

66

nice woman, tall and smart. 'I'm Mrs Billings,' she said. 'I'm very interested to hear about the horse, but aren't you going to find it difficult to keep him?'

'Oh, I'll manage somehow.' His tone said, 'Leave it to me,' and she smiled at him and asked, 'Would you like a cup of coffee?'

He hesitated a moment before saying. 'Yes, please. Yes, I would. I . . . I was so bothered this morning that I didn't have anything before coming out, but since the polis brought the letter to the stables I've been as hungry as a horse.' He laughed, and Mrs Billings laughed and Anna laughed; then, his face straight, he said quickly, 'Oh, I wasn't hinting at anything, just a drink.'

Mrs Billings's eyes twinkled as she looked down at him. Then she said, 'Come into the kitchen and I'll see what I can get you.'

'Oh, please no; I wasn't meaning . . .'

'I know what you were not meaning,' said Mrs Billings.

He looked at the girl now. She was laughing, and he felt himself going all hot and bothered. Then he went past her and followed Mrs Billings into the hall and down the passage and into the kitchen.

It was a big kitchen, all yellow and white paint with red tiles covering the floor, and he thought this was the kind of kitchen his mam would like. Not that their kitchen was bad. His dad painted it every year and his mam was always putting new curtains up all round the house. In a way he was quite proud of his home. But you could move around in a kitchen like this.

'Sit down.' Mrs Billings pointed to a chair near a long trestle table; then, almost in as short a time as it takes to tell, she had placed before him a blue mug full of hot steaming coffee, and two bacon sandwiches. He felt embarrassed eating the sandwiches but, as he had said, he was hungry.

When Mrs Billings went out of the room he looked at the girl. She was sitting on the edge of a table near the window swinging her legs. She said to him, 'Which is your favourite animal?'

Which was his favourite animal? He hadn't thought about it. He liked dogs; he would have had a dog if his mother would have let him keep one. 'Dogs, I suppose,' he said.

'Not horses?'

'Well, I haven't had much experience with horses; nor with dogs for that matter, but dogs are usually easier to handle so to speak.'

'But you like The Gladiator?'

'Oh aye. Oh aye, I like him.'

She slid off the table and came and sat down opposite to him and said with deep seriousness, 'I love horses. I'm potty about horses.'

'Oh yes,' he said politely. Then, 'Have you got a horse?' he asked her.

'No, no. You can't keep a horse in the town, can you? Well, what I mean is, unless he's a working horse like Mr Prodhurst's, or unless you've got stables and somewhere to exercise him; but privately you couldn't.'

'No, no, I suppose not.'

A silence fell between them and in it Joe became more embarrassed because she would keep staring at him.

On the sound of a door being opened and voices coming from the hall she jumped up and said, 'Here's Father now.'

Mr Billings came into the room followed by his wife. 'Hello there,' he said. 'What's this I'm hearing?'

Hastily Joe pulled the letter from his pocket and, handing it to Mr Billings, said, 'He left him to me, The Gladiator. The polis found it among his things.'

Mr Billings took the letter and after reading it he shook his head slowly, then said, 'Well, really I can't see that this is going to make much difference.'

'What do you mean?' It wasn't only a question, but a defensive statement, and Mr Billings sat down at the table and looked towards the stove where Mrs Billings was pouring out some coffee. He waited until the mug was in his hand before he said, 'How much do you think it takes to keep a horse for a week?'

Joe blinked, then said, 'Well, about ten shillings?'

'Double it and a bit more and you'll be nearer the mark,' said Mr Billings, 'much nearer the mark. And how much do you think his stabling's going to cost you?'

'Stabling?'

'Yes, his stable has to be paid for, it's part of the house. I think if I'm right the old man was paying twenty-two and sixpence a week for the house and stable, and that was cheap. And he only got it for that because the place is condemned. All those factories are due for demolition shortly. Now how long will six pounds last you at twenty-two and sixpence a week for the stabling and at least a pound a week, and I say at least, for his food? Are you prepared to pay out two pounds a week in three weeks' time say?'

When Joe didn't answer, Mr Billings repeated, 'Are you?'

'I only get fifteen shillings a week pocket money,' said Joe.

'Well, are you prepared to spend your pocket money on him?'

'Yes, yes, I would if that was enough. I could likely feed him because my mother might help me, but . . . but it's the rent.'

'You'd only be requiring the stable, wouldn't you?'

They all turned and looked at Mrs Billings. She was doing something at the table under the window and she had her back to them.

'Lucy!' There was a note of censure in Mr Billings' voice, and she said, 'Well, I just thought. Who's the agent, do you know?'

Mr Billings drained the remainder of his coffee, then said, 'Benson used to be, but he's a hard nut and as long as that place's occupied he'll want the full rent.'

'But if the place was empty tomorrow he wouldn't get any rent at all, not if it's condemned; he wouldn't be allowed to re-let.'

Joe watched Mr Billings get to his feet. He appeared slightly angry as he looked towards his wife. Then Joe looked at the girl. Her eyes were bright as they darted back and forwards between her parents.

Mr Billings now turned to Joe again and said

slowly, 'I appreciate the fact that you'd like to keep the old horse, but the most sensible thing to do would be to let things take their course, as has been arranged.'

'Oh no, Father, no!'

'Now Anna, you be quiet.'

'You said it couldn't be done until after Christmas anyway. He ... he could think it over.' Again they were looking at Mrs Billings.

'Yes, there's that.' Mr Billings nodded down at Joe. 'It would have been impossible to have had him taken away today, all the places are closed until after Christmas. The earliest would have been the day after Boxing Day. That gives you about four days. Well now, during that time you will gain some experience of what it entails just looking after him, besides the financial side. He needs care and attention, and this mightn't be too difficult when you're on holiday, but you're at work, aren't you?'

'Yes, I'm in the shipyard.'

'What on?'

'I'm going to be a marine plumber. I go to the Technical College an' all.'

'Well now, what with work and study there's not going to be much time left for seeing to a horse, is there?'

'I could help, Father.'

'ANNA!'

'I could Father, couldn't I, Mother?'

Mrs Billings made no answer to her daughter; she had contributed her share to Joe's cause and she knew when to keep quiet.

'Well I could.' Anna was looking at Joe. 'We've got nearly three weeks' holiday, and even

71

when I'm at school I could give an hour in the evenings. Oh—' she shook her head at her father – 'I won't skip my homework.'

Mr Billings drew in a long audible breath; then saying to Joe, 'Come along,' he marched out of the kitchen, and Joe, about to follow him, turned first to Mrs Billings and said, 'Thanks, Mrs ... Mrs Billings for the coffee and that,' and Mrs Billings smiled at him and said, 'It's been very nice meeting you, Joe.'

Then Joe looked at the girl, and behind her father's back she gave him the victory sign.

Eeh! thought Joe, here was another cheeky monkey. He bet she was spoilt.

Mr Billings was standing at the front door. He said firmly, 'Carry on for the next few days; then look me up and tell me what you've decided. But you know what I think. You know what I advise. It'll be the best for everybody in the long run. Good-bye, Joe.'

'Good-bye, Mr Billings.' Joe's voice was very small.

As he walked away up the street he felt weighed down with responsibility. As Mr Billings had said, he had four days to try it out, but in the meantime he would have to think about provisions for The Gladiator over the holidays. There was plenty of bedding but he'd need more seed hay just in case The Gladiator got his appetite back. And then he'd have to get in a few stale loaves and some carrots and a couple of cabbages.

Of a sudden he thought. And it's Mr Prodhurst's birthday, Christmas Eve. On this an overwhelming sense of loneliness assailed him and he found himself wishing he had company, somebody he could talk to about The Gladiator and the tasks that lay ahead. His mother wouldn't listen, not to this; she might fork out a few shillings to help him, but she wouldn't be in sympathy with him over this matter. Nor would his dad.

Willie! Aye, he'd go along and tell Willie, and ten to one he'd cheer him up.

# *Five*

'Stop laughin'.'

'Aw, but, man.'

'I've told you, stop laughin', or I'll land you one.'

Willie looked from Joe's set face to the horse standing with its head hanging, its shoulder bones probing upwards and its whole aspect dismal in the extreme, and he rubbed the side of his hand across his nose, shook his head and turned away. And after a moment he confronted Joe again. His face straight now but laughter still deep in his eyes, he said, 'You're b . . . bonkers, barmy, up the p . . . pole and over the wall to keep him.'

'Aye, well, I'm all that in your way of seeing it, and a bit more in other folks' I suppose. But you can get this into your napper, I'm going to keep him as long as I can.'

'Well, you said Mr Billings told you what it would cost . . .'

'I don't care what Mr Billings told me; I'm tellin' you I'm going to hang on to him as long as I can.'

'You'd be more in pocket if you let him go to the kn . . . knacker's yard, you'd get quite a bit for him . . .'

'Shut up, Willie, will you! Shut your stupid mouth.'

'Now look here, Joe.' Willie's tone was huffy now. 'You asked me to come round. I was on me way to me Aunt Lizzie's, I'll get it in the neck from me mother for not going there.'

Joe bit on his lip and walked over to The Gladiator and, stroking his neck slowly, he said to Willie, 'I'm sorry, man, but I don't know which end of me's up at the moment.'

He stooped now and picked up a carrot and held it against The Gladiator's mouth. The horse's upper lip moved from its teeth, and he gave one nibble at the carrot, chewed for a moment, then shook his head, and Joe said, 'He won't eat; he knows the old man's gone.'

'That's daft an' all,' said Willie, nearing the stall.

' 'Tisn't daft.'

'All right, all right, don't start bawling again. You'll make yourself as hoarse as the horse if you don't watch out.' He was laughing at his play on words, but Joe didn't laugh with him. He had gone to Willie to be cheered up but he couldn't stand him laughing at The Gladiator.

He said, 'I'm going to muck him out, clean out the stable and sort out them books in there. They should bring in a few shillings. Will you give me a hand?'

'Ah, I can't, man; I've got me good things on.'

'They're not your good things.' Joe's voice was scornful. 'But go on, get yourself away; I wouldn't have your help if you went on your knees. And don't you come huntin' me up again

75

when you're at a loose end. And wait till we get back to work, wait till you want to know anything. And then at the college ...' He wagged his finger up in Willie's face.

'When you're stuck, when that big, laughin' thick head of yours cannot understand the questions, wait till then ... Get out!'

'Ah, man, don't be like ...'

'Get out, I tell you, else you'll get The Gladiator's visiting card all over your ... good things.' He stressed the last two words.

When the door banged behind Willie Joe leant against the side of the stall. He had felt bad enough when he had left Mr Billings's house but that feeling was nothing compared to the overpowering sense of aloneness that was filling him now. It was as if he had suddenly found himself on a barren island, and there wasn't a soul on it, and there never would be, except The Gladiator and himself.

The horse now lifted its head and neighed softly, and Joe, going to him, stroked his muzzle and said, 'There, there, it's all right, boy. It's all right.' Then looking up into his face he said firmly, 'I'm goin' to tell you something. I'm more determined now than ever to keep you. I don't care what they say, any of 'em, me mam or dad, or Mr Billings, or that fool just gone, I'm goin' to keep you, so don't worry your head, lad. Don't worry your head.'

The Gladiator now nuzzled him and made the sound that he used to make to Mr Prodhurst and it warmed Joe. As there was no one to see him he put his face against the horse's cheek and whispered, 'No matter what you look like, you're mine.'

*

Joe couldn't remember exactly what he had done last Christmas Day but one thing was certain, he hadn't got up a half past seven to walk through the frozen streets to feed and muck out a horse.

His mother had called from the bedroom, 'You're not going out without any breakfast and I'm not getting up yet; go back to bed for half an hour,' and he had called back to her. 'I'll be back about nine.'

When he had returned home she had looked at him hopelessly and said, 'Boy, you're a lunatic.'

'Well, as long as I know, I won't get any high ideas about meself, will I?'

He thought he heard a chuckle come from the direction of the scullery but when his father entered the kitchen his face was straight and he said, 'Your mother's right, you are a lunatic.'

Joe made no retort to this remark because there was something heartening about it. His father had said, 'Your mother's right,' he was taking her part, and he hadn't spoken like that about her for goodness knows how long. He hadn't said lately, 'Where's your mother?' For so long it had been, 'Where's she?'

Joe looked from one to the other. He had been so taken up with Mr Prodhurst dying and The Gladiator he hadn't noticed there was a change in the house. They weren't openly friendly, but there was a different feeling between them from that which had existed for months past. Because of this he dared to say to his father, 'You wouldn't care to come and help me muck out later on, would you?'

'What!'

When his mother turned away he knew that she was trying not to laugh, and he experienced a

77

momentary feeling of happiness and said, 'I'm hungry.'

'As a...'

'No, not as a horse, Dad.' Now his mother actually did laugh as he ended, 'But as two Joe Darlings.'

'You'll want two eggs with your bacon then?' said his mother.

'Aye, and a double helpin' of fried bread, or anything else that's goin'.'

'Listen to him.' She jerked her head as she went into the scullery, and his father said, 'That's horse sense.'

At this point Joe wanted to say, 'Aw, shut up, man.' But that would put a damper on the new atmosphere in the kitchen and he didn't want to do anything to spoil that. But the atmosphere was slightly strained again when, after breakfast, his mother cleared the table, and, as was usual, they exchanged their Christmas presents.

Joe was frankly delighted at the wrist watch. It was a joint present from his parents. And at the sweater from his mother and the gloves from his father.

When his mother opened her parcel and found a smart jersey suit she looked at her husband and said, 'It's beautiful. Thanks.'

Joe watched his father turn to the fireplace and stub out a cigarette, saying, 'If it doesn't fit they'll change it.'

'Oh, it'll fit all right, you've always bought me things that fit me.'

There was a short silence before Mr Darling opened his parcel, and when he saw a fancy grey waistcoat he said, 'Coo! fancy me in this.'

'You said you would like one.'

'Aye, yes, I did.' He nodded at her. 'But it's going to take some courage to wear it at the club.'

'No doubt you'll find it.' It was a quiet remark and he laughed and said, 'Aye.'

'Put it on, Dad.'

When Mr Darling was attired in the waistcoat they exclaimed how smart it was. Then they opened Joe's presents. There was a pair of silk stockings and a brooch for his mother, a pair of socks and fifty cigarettes for his father, and they acted as if he had given them the crown jewels.

'You must be broke,' his father said to him, and he answered, 'Oh, I'm all right.'

Shortly after this, Mr Darling, looking at his wife, said, 'I'd better go up top,' and she, looking back at him, said, 'Yes, and take her this.' She handed him a parcel.

He said now, 'Will I ask her down?'

'But she's going to your cousin Lily's for her dinner.'

'I mean after, later on.'

'You can.'

Mr Darling, now turning to Joe, said, 'What about you?' and Joe replied, 'I'll be up in a minute with her present.'

When Joe was alone with his mother he gazed at her and asked softly, 'Things panning out, Mam?'

Mrs Darling sat down with a slight plop on a chair and, joining her hands tightly in her lap, she said, 'I hope so, Joe, I hope so. But . . . but I don't know yet.'

'You don't know?' He screwed his face up at her. 'What do you mean?'

'Well, it's like this.' She leant towards him. 'Now you're not to say a word to anybody, do you hear?'

He waited.

'There's some people who live near the bottom of Ocean Road. The man works in the hospital here. Well, we're practically on the doorstep, and as he wants to be near his work and we want to get away from' – she turned her eyes towards the ceiling – 'we're going to exchange houses. Now listen.' She nodded her head quickly at him. 'There's nothing settled yet. Your dad and the man are just talking about it, but it would be a solution: once we're away from her everything would be as it was afore.'

After a moment of complete silence Joe asked. 'What kind of a house is it?'

'I haven't seen it yet but it's in James Street. They're not bad houses round there. I think they're bigger than this, and I could do with another room. I'd like some place where we could eat, you know, separate from this.' She made a gesture with her hands. 'But the main thing is, your grannie is not to know until we're gone.'

'Won't she find out?'

'Not until the furniture is going out, if I can help it, and then she can't do anything about it.'

'I see,' he said. And he did see. But somehow he wasn't happy about it; it was sort of underhand, springing it on his grannie at the last minute. But she deserved what she was getting. Oh aye. But still . . .

His mother now, putting her hand on his, said, 'You were right that time not to choose between us, quite right. It steadied me sort of, because you know' – she lowered her eyes – 'if you had said you'd come with me I'd have been off like a shot.'

Again he looked at her in silence.

She now got briskly to her feet and gathering up the Christmas paper and wrappings from the table she said, 'What are you going to do with yourself after you've been upstairs?' then added on a laugh, 'Oh, don't tell me. But mind—' she pointed at him – 'you be back at one for your dinner else you'll wonder which cuddy kicked you.'

She was laughing heartily at her joke and he joined in. For he had better, he thought, get used to such jokes as soon as possible because for the rest of his life he would have jokes thrown at him about horses, cuddies, and nags.

An hour later he was shovelling snow from the path that encircled the old iron when the gate was pushed open and he straightened his back to see the girl standing there.

'Hello,' she said.

'Hello,' he answered.

'Merry Christmas,' she said.

'Same to you,' he answered.

'How is he?' she asked.

'All right, I think. A bit better. He ate a mouthful or two, not enough to keep him going but at least he tried.'

'Can I see him?'

' 'Course. Come on in.'

Anna stood looking at The Gladiator for a full minute before she said, 'Poor thing.'

She seemed sort of upset and Joe said, 'He's all right. If he once starts eating he'll be all right.'

'He's got no flesh on him.'

'He's big made,' said Joe.

'But he shouldn't look like this,' she said.

'He's eighteen years old,' said Joe.

'There's one at the Palmerston Stables and he's twenty-four. He's well covered and still trots about . . . I see what Father means.' She turned and gazed at Joe, and he replied angrily, 'I don't care what your father says or anybody else I'm goin' to keep him.'

She smiled at him now. 'I'm glad,' she said.

'Well, what are you on about then?'

'What do you mean?'

'Saying you know what your father meant.'

'Well, I do. Father says this is no life for a horse; and like other people, horses need company.'

'Well, he has me; I'll be in and out.'

'That isn't like him having Mr Prodhurst. He was with him all the time.'

'You're a comfort,' said Joe. 'You get better as you keep talkin'.'

She did not appear annoyed at his attitude but said quietly, 'I'm with you.'

'You sound like it.'

'I am, I'm telling you.' Her voice was loud now. 'I even got Father to look in yesterday afternoon on Mr Benson, the agent . . . at least it was nearly like that. We were passing the office and Mr Benson was locking up and I asked dad to speak to him.'

'You did? What happened?'

'Well, he said he would see. There's one thing I think you can be sure of though. If you don't use the house I don't think you'll have to pay for it.'

'Oh, I don't want the house. Good Lord, no. Just the stable here.'

'Anyway, we'll have to wait and see; we won't know until after the holidays.'

Joe stared at her. She looked ordinary. He wouldn't have noticed her twice if he had passed her in the street. There seemed nothing about her until she opened her mouth. She had a lovely voice. And then when he came to think about it her eyes were nice, kindly sort of; and her hair wasn't bad. He watched her go and stroke The Gladiator's cheek and he thought with some surprise, she isn't afraid of him. Willie had been afraid to go near him.

She turned and looked towards Joe now as she asked, 'Will you let me help with him?'

Joe hesitated. Help from Willie he would have welcomed, but this was a lass.

She said, 'I don't care what I do.'

He stalled by saying, 'What about your folks?'

'Oh, they won't mind. I could stay now and give you a hand. We're not having dinner until four o'clock, so I've got plenty of time.'

Christmas dinner at four o'clock! That was a funny time to have it. He said, 'We're having ours at one; you can help till then if you like.'

'Good-o!' she said. 'I'll help you finish the path, then we'll clean him out and walk him round.'

And that's what they did. And then they put clean straw in the stall and coaxed him to eat a little bread. When all this was finished Joe saw to his amazement that it was half past one.

Looking at her, he cried, 'Coo! lor! I'll get it in the neck.' He almost pushed her through the gate, where, after locking up, he took a brusque farewell of her and ran slithering all the way home.

And he did get it in the neck.

# *Six*

'It isn't everybody who's got a horse, you know.'

'No, by, you're right there. They say he's goin' to enter him for the Derby.'

'Is he now? Well! Well! What do you think the odds will be?'

'Oh, I should say about five thousand to one.'

There was a burst of smothered laughter followed by a silence, which Joe, on the other side of the partition, knew would be given over to winks and nudges; then the voices started again. 'Fine name that for a horse, The Gladiator.'

'Aye, never heard owt like it, The Gladiator. Eeh! sounds grand, doesn't it?'

'But mind, from what I've heard of him and the way his bones are set in steps and stairs he could be used for an escalator.'

Another burst of laughter, louder this time. Joe grimly looked at his watch. Two minutes to go before the buzzer went and then the noise of the hammering would shut out their voices. They were grown men, yet they were worse than the lads, but it was a lad he had to blame for this. He looked to where Willie was seated some distance away. Big mouth, anything to get a laugh. The whole ship knew about The Gladiator. Men he had never spoken to nodded at him and said. 'Hello there, lad, can you give us a tip?' Even Mr Ripley had said, 'You riding him yourself, Joe?'

He was surprised at Mr Ripley. And then later when he had been giving Willie Styles the length of his tongue Mr Ripley had come upon them and said, 'Now, now, don't put all the blame on Styles; you must remember that Taggerine Ted's horse was well known in the town. He was a joke years ago.'

A joke: a horse, a poor dumb animal. He'd like to scuttle every man jack of them. He had a momentary picture of the ship in the river and himself pulling out a gigantic plug, and he told himself he wouldn't bat an eyelid when he saw them drown; that is all except Harry Farthing.

Funny about Harry Farthing; he hadn't ragged him once about The Gladiator. He'd seen Harry laughing with the other fellows but it could have been about anything; yet knowing what he had been like he would have expected him to be the worst on the ship, but since that business of the name signing he had left off him. And that was something to be thankful for. Aye, yes.

Looking back to life before Christmas, Joe thought he mustn't have had a worry in the world then. Of course there had been the trouble at home, but that was different somehow. Now nearly every minute of his waking hours seemed to be taken up with the incessant worry about money. In spite of Mr Billings getting him the stable for twelve shillings a week it was going to take nigh on two pounds a week altogether to support The Gladiator.

He had supplemented the six pounds that Mr Prodhurst had left by selling his books. He had got four pounds for the lot; he had enough money to carry on for another three weeks but after that it would be entirely up to him, and stretch it as he would he couldn't turn fifteen shillings into thirty-five, never mind two pounds.

Anna had said that her mother would keep The Gladiator going with green stuff and carrots and bread, and he could accept that, but not the half-a-crown from her pocket money that she had offered to subscribe. He was made to wonder how he would have got on these past ten days without Anna Billings. She was a good kid; she was the only one who had stood by him, really stood by him.

The buzzer blew and the work began and as he went to his section one of the wise-cracking men shouted to him, 'Don't look so down in the mouth, Joe; ten to one he'll make your fortune yet. Stranger things have happened.'

Joe glared at the man. Lord, how he wished he was big. One thing he was determined to do. Once he got his life organized he was going to go in for the boxing classes at the college club. By! he'd show them. He now had a picture of himself pinning Mr Rice, the man who had just ribbed him, against the bulkheads. He could hear himself shouting, 'Say that again! Go on, say that again!'

And the chipping didn't end in the shipyard. Willie had been opening his mouth in the college too and fellows he had never spoken to before called to him with such remarks as Mr Ripley had used, 'Are you riding him yourself, little 'un? You could, you know.' Even the tutor, Mr Guest, broached the subject. 'What's this I'm hearing, Joe? Someone's left you a horse?'

When Joe continued to stare down at his book the jocular note went out of Mr Guest's voice and he said, 'Don't let it get you down. If you want my opinion, I think you're doing a very courageous thing in keeping the beast. It isn't easy, is it?'

Joe looked up at the master and it was a moment before he said 'No, it isn't easy; but I can't see anything very funny about it, Sir.'

'No,' said Mr Guest, 'you won't be able to from where you're standing. But I don't think the old fellow should have saddled you with him.'

'Mr Prodhurst was a nice man, he was a good man; I talked to him a lot before he died.'

'Did you?'

'Yes. I got to know him well. That's . . . that's why he left me The Glad . . . his horse.'

'Well, horse or no horse,' said Mr Guest now, 'he's not interfering with your work, you're coming up to standard again.'

'Thank you, Sir.'

'Keep it up.'

'I'll try, Sir.'

You would have thought, mused Joe when he was alone once more, that people would have something else to think about, and they must be very hard up for something to laugh at when they went all hilarious over an old horse. The vast majority of people hadn't much sense, at least they hadn't a sense of what was right and proper.

What was more, he concluded, The Gladiator,

no matter how he looked, was an animal of high intelligence who understood everything that was said to him; it was a sort of sixth sense, horse sense, if you like. For days after Mr Prodhurst had died he would hardly eat anything, but on the day following the funeral he had eaten his first square meal, and what was more he had bucked up since then. He was even getting sprightly. Last Sunday he had pawed at the earth in the yard and tossed up his head and neighed as if he was glad to be alive.

It was as he had stood smiling at him that the gate had opened and the strange man had come into the yard and looked at them. He had said to the man. 'Do you want Mr Prodhurst? I'm sorry, he's dead,' and the man had answered, 'No, I wasn't looking for Mr Prodhurst.' And he had stood there staring at The Gladiator. Then he had turned abruptly and walked out, leaving Joe feeling distinctly uneasy. And the feeling had stayed with him for days afterwards.

There was yet another thing troubling Joe. It was to do with the exchange of houses. As it was now he could run from his home to the stable in ten minutes, but if they went to live down the bottom end of Ocean Road he wouldn't be able to do it in under forty minutes, and taking the bus would be out of the question because that would cost money. Yet he knew he mustn't voice his objections to the move because this might put a spanner in the works. The feeling between his mother and father was balanced so delicately at present that it could swing either forward into happiness or back to where it had been for months past.

Some fellows grew to be six foot tall, got a gold Olympic medal, married a multi-millionaire's daughter and bought up the entire docks. Other fellows just had problems. So went the saying in the yard.

Well, he was the fellow who just had problems.

# Seven

The snow had gone. The morning was dry and bright. The sun was shining, the sky was high and even The Gladiator was being fooled into the impression that it was spring.

'Look at him!' cried Joe. 'I've never seen him so frisky.'

'I'm sure he's putting on weight,' said Anna. She was looking at The Gladiator with pride as he walked around the path. 'You know something?'

'What?' Joe wasn't looking at Anna, he had his eyes on The Gladiator. That was until she said, 'We should take him out, to the common. The Parmeson Stables take their horses there.'

'You mean take him through the town? All that way?'

'Why not?'

Joe watched The Gladiator approaching with his ponderous, gangling gait, and for a moment he saw the animal as others would see him, the folks in the street.

'You're not ashamed of him, are you?'

'No! No!' His denial was high. 'But it's just that you don't see people taking horses through the streets nowadays, and all the traffic about.'

91

'There wouldn't be much traffic today, it's Sunday.'

That was true. But to take him all that way, along by the Chichester, through Westoe.

'Come on,' she said; 'he would love it. Poor thing, he never gets out. He never sees anything but the stable and this yard. What do you say?'

She was just a lass. He could shut her up – after all it was his horse – but she wasn't just any lass, she was Anna, and she cared for The Gladiator nearly as much as he himself did, and what he had to face up to was that if she hadn't stood by him he would have been absolutely on his own and probably sunk. He jerked his head now and said, 'Well, have it your own way; but ... but what if he takes fright and gallops off?'

She now smiled at him quizzically as she said, 'For my part I'd like to see him gallop off.'

'Would you now?' he nodded at her. 'Well, here's one that wouldn't. I can't see meself galloping along Westoe after him.'

'I can.'

He was forced to laugh; then brusquely he added, 'Well, if we're going to take him, let's get moving. He'll want reins and things.'

'I'll get them.' She was running into the stable. 'And this'll be an opportunity for him to wear his blanket.'

'Yes,' he said. 'Oh yes, it will an' all.'

She had brought him a blanket. It was an old one, but it was a real horse blanket with a fancy coloured edge.

From the moment they opened the gates and led The Gladiator into the road, the horse knew where he was going. His step quickened and he tossed his head, and twice he moved so quickly that the blanket slipped from his back.

There was hardly any traffic about and very few people. The church-goers hadn't yet come out of the church, and the bars hadn't yet opened; for the rest, the community seemed to be indoors, and as Joe approached the common his spirits lightened. It had been easy, a piece of cake. He'd do this every Sunday. He patted The Gladiator and said, 'You're nearly there, boy,' and The Gladiator knew he was nearly there.

The common in parts was bare, and still hard from an overnight frost, and but for a man and woman and a dog in the far distance they had the big stretch of open ground to themselves.

'Come on, trot!' cried Anna, and The Gladiator needed no second bidding.

Joe had never seen the horse move at anything quicker than a walk and when he saw him break into a trot and the blanket slip from him again, for only the second time during their acquaintance did he feel inclined to laugh at his friend.

Every bone in The Gladiator's body seemed to be aiming to force itself out through his skin. More than ever now he looked comical, if a great mass of skin and bone could look comical. Joe was running at one side of him, egging him on, laughing freely with Anna, both crying, 'That's it, boy!'

After trotting half-way across the common The Gladiator's pace dropped to a walk again and Joe, gasping and still laughing, patted him on the neck as he cried, 'Wasn't that great? Didn't you enjoy that?'

For an hour they kept him walking and trotting,

and then they started on their return journey home.

Where before it had appeared that the town was almost empty of people, now it seemed as if everybody had flung their doors wide and had poured out into the streets. As they made their way down Dean Road towards the Chichester the pavements were full of people and the roads full of vehicles.

When they took the road to Laygate, off which they had to turn to reach Brick Fields Gate, they encountered a group of boys idling in the entrance of a back lane. A very large horse and two comparatively small people seemed to be just what they were waiting for, and they began to enjoy themselves.

Walking along the pavement within an arm's length of Anna one cried to the others, 'What is it?'

'It's Taggerine Ted's horse.'

'No, man, it's no horse. Look at its humps; it's a dromedary.'

The loud yells and laughter brought The Gladiator's head bobbing, and one of the boys cried, 'It's alive, from the neck up. Look, it's alive.'

'Has he escaped from the circus, little 'un?'

Whether it was the insult to The Gladiator, or the reference to his height, Joe stopped abruptly. Pulling The Gladiator to a halt and facing the half dozen boys, he yelled back at them, 'Watch it! Now mind, I'm tellin' you, watch it.'

'Listen to him! Coo! Him not the size of three pennorth of copper, an' listen to him!'

'You'll not only hear me,' said Joe now, 'you'll

94

feel me hand, and me boot if you don't get about your business.'

The laughter now was high and derisive, but all the same the boys kept their distance and Joe, looking past The Gladiator's head towards Anna, said, 'It's all right, don't you worry.'

'I'm not,' said Anna.

'Here, change over,' he said under his breath, and he almost pulled her to the off side of the horse, and took up his position near the kerb and nearer the boys.

'I got a horse! I got a horse!' one started now, and the others took up the chant. 'He's got a horse. They've got a horse. We've all got a horse.'

The Gladiator trudged heavily on and Joe, grim faced, stared ahead, and when into his line of vision walked Willie, he thought, 'Aw, Lord, no.'

As Willie fell into step beside him, Joe knew he was in for one of his funny turns and he remained grimly silent as Willie let his eyes roam over the horse, then over the crowd on the pavement, and lastly directed them towards Anna's feet on the other side of The Gladiator. But, of course, it was Joe he addressed.

'H . . . Hello' he said, with a wide grin, 'out for a c . . . canter?'

Joe didn't pause, he kept up a steady pace; nor did he look at Willie as he said, 'No, I'm taking lessons in gliding.'

There was appreciation of this quip from the group on the pavement, and Willie joined his laughter to theirs. Then, 'Where you been?' he asked.

'To the pictures,' said Joe.

Again there was laughter from the boys. They now looked at Joe with admiration; he might be little but in their estimation he was all there.

'I'll come along with you,' said Willie now, and Joe said, 'Thanks, but I've bought a joke book, I know them all.'

Willie now stepped ahead of the horse and, looking across at Anna, said, 'He's been sw ... sw ... swallowing razor b ... blades.' Then by way of introduction he added, 'I'm his pal.'

'Oh!' said Anna.

Willie looked appreciatively at Anna. Joe hadn't let on he had a lass helping him. He was tight was Joe, and now when Joe's voice came to him, saying, 'Pal, huh!' he grinned at Anna and said, 'He's like that.'

Joe was about to retort to this when he felt The Gladiator's step check and, looking behind, he saw two of the boys hanging on The Gladiator's tail.

'Geroff!' He made a dive at them, and they jumped on to the pavement.

'Do that again and I'll call the polis, see if I don't.'

'He'll call the polis. He'll call the polis. He'll call the polis.' They took up the chant; then they stopped abruptly when Anna's voice, cool and indifferent, said, 'By the look of you you could be anything from fourteen to eighteen, but by the sound of you you must be between four and six.'

There was a pause before one of the boys said, 'Coo, aren't we high school!'

They were nearing a public house now and the main door opened and three men came out and stopped to watch their approach. At sight of one of them Joe groaned to himself again. What was the matter? What had happened that he should bump into them all at one go? The tallest of the men now confronting them was Harry Farthing.

'Hello there,' he said. 'Out for a stroll?' There was a smile on his face but when, before Joe could answer, one of the boys yelled, 'No, he's had it at the pictures to see Champion, The Wonder Horse,' Harry Farthing turned on the boy and said, 'Well, mind you don't suddenly find yourself in the pictures with The Wonder Horse's hoof in your backside.'

The laugh was turned against the boy now and Harry Farthing bawled, 'Get yourselves away afore I nobble the lot of you.'

'You and who else?' one of the group shouted but made sure to back away as he did so.

When Harry Farthing made a dive towards them, they all scattered, yelling and jeering.

Joe looked at Harry Farthing. He couldn't really make him out. Of all the people, he told himself, he wouldn't want to meet this morning he was the main one, for he couldn't imagine the big fellow's gratitude stretching to such lengths as would prevent him guffawing at The Gladiator.

But Harry didn't guffaw; what he did was to join the cavalcade, and explain to his companions about Joe and The Gladiator. 'Ted Prodhurst's horse you know,' he said. 'Joe here used to help him and he left it to him.'

'Aye,' the men nodded, seemingly taking the cue from Harry and aiming to keep their faces straight.

'Joe here's takin' him on. It's a big job; costs

97

something to keep a horse these days. Think you'll be able to manage it, Joe?'

Joe swallowed hard before he said, 'I'll have a good try, Harry.'

'Aye, I bet you will. Knowing you I bet you'll have a good try.'

Joe wished he would get himself away, he and his companions, and take Willie with them; but there was no fear of Willie leaving now that he had seen Anna. Oh no; he would be out to create an impression, the big ha-ha impression.

They reached the gate at last and when Joe unlocked it and led the horse through the yard into the stable the rest followed.

'Not a bad stable, is it?' said Harry Farthing, and his companions repeated parrot like, 'No, not a bad stable.' Then looking at the heap of tangled iron in the middle of the yard Harry said, 'Why don't you get rid of the junk, Joe?'

'Who'd want that?'

'Oh, plenty. I bet Boyle's would take it. I reckon there's twenty quid's worth there or more.'

'You think so?' Joe's interest was now aroused.

'And there's bits of lead among it, look.' He picked up a length of piping. 'You know what lead costs. It's a wonder somebody hasn't been over the wall and sorted this lot out. I'd get rid of it, Joe, if I were you.'

'Where's Boyle's?' asked Joe.

'You know, the yard beyond the bottom dock.'

'Oh, that place.'

'Look, I come round that way to work, I'll call in and tell them if you like.'

'Would you?'

98

'Aye, no trouble. I bet you could do with the money . . . How much have you got left?'

Joe felt his temper take a leap; then he clamped down on his lip. 'Oh, enough,' he said grimly.

'What do you mean by enough? Five pounds? Fifty pounds?'

Joe closed his eyes and jerked his head to one side, and Harry, taking off his cap and thrusting his hand into his pocket, said, 'well, there's ten bob towards his feed. What about you, Jack?'

'What!' exclaimed one of his companions; then hesitated perceptibly before putting a half-a-crown into Harry's hat.

'Come on, come on,' said Harry; 'double it, man.'

'You're askin' somethin', aren't you?'

'Go on.'

The man added another half-crown and his companion followed suit with five shillings, and now Harry was holding the hat out towards Willie, and Willie, grinning, said, 'What, me?'

'Aye, you.'

'But you know what I g . . . get.'

'Aye, I know what you get and you can afford half a dollar. Come on, fork out.'

'Aw, man.' The smile slid from Willie's face, but he put his hand into his pocket and when he put a shilling into the hat, Harry said, 'Mind you don't hurt yourself. You know what you are, all gas and no gizzard.'

During this performance Joe and been standing near the stable door. He felt angry and embarrassed, yet at the same time grateful in an odd sort of way to Harry Farthing, and when Harry held out the hat to him, saying. 'There you are, one guinea,' Joe took it and said, 'It's good of you, Harry,' and nodding to the men he said, 'Thanks.' But he didn't thank Willie. As soon as they were gone he'd give him his shilling back, you see if he didn't.

'I won't forget about Boyle's,' said Harry loudly as they took their leave, and Joe, going to the gate with them, said again, 'Thanks, Harry, thanks.' He noticed that Harry Farthing looked pleased, sort of happy. He had never seen him like this before. Who could tell, perhaps he would get to like him.

When he returned to the stable Anna was rubbing The Gladiator down and Willie was standing watching her. 'Here, there's your shilling.' Joe thrust the coin at him and Willie, on an airy laugh, said, 'What's up with you, man? I don't want that.'

'Take it and get yourself away.'

'I've come to give you a hand.'

'What!' Joe gave a mirthless laugh. 'In your good clothes? Don't come it, man. I know why you're stayin'; you know why you're stayin'.' Joe cast a glance towards Anna, then, cocking his head to one side and his tone altering, he said, 'I wouldn't think about you getting your clothes messed up, but you can come round the morrow night and give me a hand, because Anna here will be at school and she can only come twice a week because she's got her homework to do. It's a date then?'

'Oh, the morrow night? That's different.' Willie thrust his hands in his pocket and walked to the door of the stable. 'It's homework for me an' all; you know it is.'

'You know what you are, Willie Styles,' Joe marched up to his so-called friend, and glared up at him. 'You're what is known as an opportunist.'

'What?'

'You heard, an opportunist. Well, if you're not comin' the morrow night you're not coming any other time.'

'An' you know what you are, Joe Darling, you're nothin' but a b ... b ... bad tempered little sq ... squirt, that's what you are. An' I'll tell you something else. I'm finished with you, and don't expect me to w ... wait for you in the morning.'

'Coo!' Joe's breath was taken away for a moment but he shouted as Willie went through the gate. 'You've got your facts mixed up, haven't you? But it's OK with me. And good riddance.'

Joe turned back into the stable, and there was Anna standing looking at him, and she said quietly, 'Is he really your friend?'

Joe shrugged his shoulders as he replied, 'Sort of, I suppose.'

'You were pretty rough with him.'

'Oh, you don't know him; he never does anything for anybody except make them laugh, and he knows he can and he plays on it. He gets on my wick.'

'I didn't think he was bad.' She turned towards The Gladiator again.

Joe stood still looking at her. Girls were all alike, there wasn't a pin to choose between them. It had been the same with Jessica Walsh, the daughter of the farmer where they had camped last summer in the Northumbrian hills. She had thought Willie was fun an' all; she hadn't bothered with Matty or him, nor looked the side they were on . . . Matty!

The name was like a bell ringing loudly in his head. Matty was on a farm, and round the farm were fields and fields and fields. Joe now let his gaze rest on The Gladiator and he moved slowly towards him, muttering, 'Matty! up on that farm, with all those fields.'

'What did you say?' asked Anna.

'I said Matty, Matty Doolin. He was a pal of mine. He works on a farm in Northumberland; there's miles and miles of empty land all around him.'

Anna now came and stood by his side and she laughed at him as she said, 'You're not proposing to walk The Gladiator to this farm, are you?'

'No,' said Joe; 'don't be daft. But it just set me thinking.' He took his eyes from her and looked at The Gladiator again as he said, 'I haven't seen Matty for months. I miss him, we were great pals. I think I'll write him a letter.'

It was a momentous decision.

# *Eight*

Joe didn't write Matty the letter for the simple
reason that he kept putting it off, he hated writing letters. But three weeks later there came
a Saturday morning when he knew something
would have to be done or they all would have their
way and The Gladiator would go to the knacker's
yard.

He had enough money left for one week's feed
and rent, and then he would have to depend on his
pocket money and what he could scrounge from
his mam and dad.

He was feeling very tired, not only with worry,
but with actual work. His mother was right in
one way, it was proving too much; he seemed to
be for ever dashing from the house to the stable,
or from the shipyard to the stable, and now the
whole situation looked more impossible still seen
from the point of view of their new house at the
bottom of Ocean Road, to which his mother was
taking him this afternoon.

The move had put him in a bigger quandary
than ever, so much seemed to depend on it; in
fact, the future happiness of his parents and their
remaining together as a family.

Joe looked at The Gladiator where he stood

munching hay. He seemed to be eating more than ever now. He should be glad about this but he wasn't, because actually he was shortening his life. If he couldn't find the money to go on feeding him, what then?

The Gladiator stopped eating and came towards him. This was a funny thing about the horse, Joe thought. He seemed sort of human, for whenever he himself was very worried The Gladiator would rub him with his head and nudge him with his mouth, as much as to say, 'Aw, lad, don't worry, everything will pan out.'

He said to him now, 'It's all right for you but you haven't got to find the cash. Anyway come on out for a trot round.' He led him into the yard; which now looked almost twice its original size since it had been cleared of junk. Harry Farthing had been as good as his word and Boyle's collector had called and cleared the place, but not for twenty pounds; all he had got for the scrap was four pounds, yet he knew that if Harry Farthing himself had been there he would have made a better bargain of the deal.

It was a cold grey morning but The Gladiator seemed glad enough of the fresh air, for he tossed his head and his nostrils widened and quivered.

When the back gate opened he neighed and Joe turned and saw the man again. This was the third time he had been here. Two weeks ago he had come in and Joe had asked, 'Who are you?' and the man had said, 'My name is Tellman.' That was all and then he had gone.

The man looked about the yard as he came towards him; then he said, 'You've made a clearance?'

'Aye,' said Joe stiffly.

'How are you getting on?'

'Oh, not so bad,' said Joe.

'Finding him a bit of a trial?' The man nodded towards The Gladiator, and Joe said, 'Well, yes and no. Not in himself, he's no trouble in himself, he's a good horse, but I've got to go to work you see, and I go to the Technical College and I've got homework. It takes all me time.'

'Yes, it will,' said the man. 'You finding it difficult to feed him?'

Joe looked at the man. He wasn't a workman, he looked like an office bloke, he talked like one an' all. He wondered what he was up to. Perhaps he was a member of the R.S.P.C.A. or something. Yes, that was it. He was talking more than he had done before; he was trying to find things out. Joe's answer was cautious, 'Oh, well, everything takes money you know,' he said.

'Yes, I'm well aware of that,' said the man. 'Are you thinking of keeping him?' he now asked.

'Yes, of course I am.' Joe's manner was aggressive now, but the man said calmly, 'Well, for how long?'

'I don't know ... long as I can ... till he dies.'

The man said, 'Good, good;' then he turned away and walked up the yard. He had never spoken to The Gladiator but he hadn't laughed at him either. At the gate he turned again and inclined his head towards Joe, then he was gone.

Odd bloke. Funny, queer. What business was it of his anyway? Had he anything to do with the R.S.P.C.A., or the P.D.S.A.? Those blokes were hot on animals. Of course they had to be, but they wouldn't have anything on him, he'd see to that. Yes, but how? . . .

He was still asking himself this question at three o'clock in the afternoon, only more so now as he sat in the little room in Number 10 James Street with a cup of tea in his hand. He didn't like this house; he didn't like the people who owned it; and instinctively he knew his mother didn't like the house, but also instinctively he knew she was going to come here to live.

Half an hour later as he walked up the street into Ocean Road, from out of a long silence Mrs Darling said, 'Well?' And Joe, after a pause, answered, 'Aw, Mam, what do you expect me to say? Truth is I don't like the house, nor the place, apart from the fact it's going to be impossible for me to get from there to the stable every morning unless I get up at half past five.'

'There's a solution to that,' his mother said stiffly, 'and it's got to come some day so it might as well come now. And Joe—' she cast a hard glance towards him – 'we're going to move there; it's the only way. It would be different if we could get a house anywhere else but you know we can't. This is the answer to all our problems . . . well, at least—' she nodded her head quickly – 'it's the answer to mine and your dad's because if we don't get away from your grannie it's going to be the finish of us.'

'Well, if you want to know what I think, I think it's dirty.'

'What's dirty?'

'The way you're doing it; it'll give her a shock when she finds out.'

'She'll be able to withstand that,' said Mrs Darling tartly. 'She's as hard as nails. But, look, get this straight. This wasn't my idea, it was your dad's; he's thought it out, he's done everything. This is the first time I've been down here. Well, no, I'm tellin' a lie, I walked through the street to see what it looked like on the outside. But I mean to say this is your dad's idea, not mine. And remember your grannie is his mother, not mine.'

Aye, thought Joe, that's where the trouble lay, his grannie was his dad's mother; it might have been different if she had been his mam's mother, but his mam's mother and father had been dead for years.

Joe left his mother and walked up Fowler Street and took the never ending short cuts to the stable. Again he was feeling very much alone. He hadn't realized up till this moment how much he missed Anna being around but she had gone away for the weekend with her mother. He wished he had someone to talk to, someone who understood about The Gladiator, but who besides himself and Anna saw the horse other than as a big caricature of a beast only fit to be made into dog food.

It was as he passed a telephone kiosk that the thought came to him, I could phone Matty. He paused to consider this. How much would it cost? He had to count every penny now but perhaps this was money worth spending. If the idea that had been in the back of his mind could be put into practice wouldn't this solve his problem?

He couldn't find Mr Walsh's number in the phone book and he did a lot of fumbling before he got through to the exchange and they got the number of the farm for him. When he heard the bell ringing his heart began to pound rapidly; then his face split into a wide grin as a familiar voice said, 'Hello, Mrs Walsh speaking.'

'Hello, Mrs Walsh, this is Joe, Joe Darling. Remember?'

'Oh, Joe!' Her voice was high and filled with pleasure, and she said, 'Fancy hearing you. How are you, Joe?'

'I'm all right, Mrs Walsh.'

'Oh, I suppose it's Matty you want to speak to?'

'Yes, Mrs Walsh, please.'

'Well, hang on a moment and I'll get him.'

'Hello.'

Aw, that was Matty all right, it was as if he was in the box with him. 'Hello, Matty.'

'Hello, Joe. Anything wrong?'

'Well, I'm in a bit of a fix.'

'What is it?'

'It's about a horse.'

There came Matty's deep laugh over the wire, and then he said, 'I thought you said it was about a horse.'

'Aye, I did . . . You remember Taggerine Ted's horse?'

'Who could forget that one.'

Joe looked hard at the mouthpiece before he said, 'I've got news for you, he's mine; Mr Prodhurst left him to me when he died.'

'You must be kiddin'.'

'I'm not, Matty. And another thing, he's a marvellous old beast. What I mean, he's intelligent like; he can practically talk.'

108

Again Matty's laugh came; then he said, 'I've never met anyone who owned a dog or a horse yet who didn't say it could practically talk. I've got a dog of me own now and he can speak three languages.'

'Oh, stop kiddin', Matty, I'm serious; I'm in a fix. You see the money's running out and with me pocket money and a bit over I'll just be able to feed him, but then there's the stabling and it's twelve and six a week. And apart from that we're going to have to move down to the bottom of Ocean Road and I can't see me being able to keep it up, I mean feed him afore I go to work and then dinner-time and at night an' all, and everybody's at me to have him sent to the knacker's yard, and I can't do it, Matt, I can't do it.'

There was a long pause before Matty said, 'Well, what do you want me to do, Joe?'

Joe thought it was apparent what he wanted him to do. He said now, 'I was wondering if . . . if Mr Walsh would have him out there. I would pay for him, I would pay for his keep.'

'Aw, Joe, I don't know, I can't tell you that; you'd have to ask Mr Walsh.'

'Well, could you put it to him for me?'

'Yes, yes, I could do that. But I can't say one way or the other; you see Jessica's got a pony now.'

'Oh, has she?' The excitement came over in Joe's voice. 'Then the Gladiator could be company for him.'

'The what?'

Joe again looked hard at the mouthpiece before he said, 'The Gladiator. That's what Mr Prodhurst used to call him . . . Ah, stop laughin', man. He was a grand horse at one time. You should see him.'

'You forget I have seen him, Joe; I've seen him for years.'

Joe could say nothing to this. Then in the silence Matty's voice said, 'Well, I'll do what I can. I'll drop you a line and . . .'

A precise voice on the wire now said, 'Your time is up, do you want . . . ?'

'Ta-rah, Matty!' shouted Joe.

'Ta-rah, Joe!' Back came Matty's voice.

Joe put down the receiver and went out into the street again; he didn't feel heartened at all. If it had just lain with Matty, he felt sure everything would have been all right, but Mr Walsh was a hard man. He was nice enough but he had a business-like head on him. There was one thing certain. If Mr Walsh ever saw The Gladiator before he reached the farm all hope would be gone; The Gladiator would have to be sprung on Mr Walsh, so to speak. It needed a sort of miracle and Joe knew that miracles didn't happen these days.

Matty's letter came on a Tuesday morning but Joe didn't see it until he came in from work. When his mother handed it to him he ripped off the top of the envelope and a corner of the letter in his excitement and then, after reading the single page, because Matty too hated writing letters, he looked from his mother to his father, and they were both looking at him, and it was to his father, he spoke, his words tumbling out in his excitement. 'He . . . he wants to see me . . . Mr Walsh. He said we should talk. Matty . . . Matty

110

says you can run me out if you like, all of us on Sunday. Mrs Walsh; she'll give us dinner.'

'Hold your hand a minute. Hold your hand,' said his father, getting to his feet. 'What you talking about? Run you where?'

'Mr Walsh's farm. You know where I went camping last year. Past Hexham; no, further on, Whitfield, up on the fells.'

'And he wants us to go there on Sunday?' said his father.

'Aye.'

'And it might be snowing and us get bogged down?'

'There's no snow now.'

'Not here there isn't, but up on those fells, they're never free of it in the winter.'

'Don't be daft, Dad . . .'

'Here, here!' His mother scolded now and he returned to her and said, 'Well, what I mean is, it isn't up in Scotland and it isn't that far up the fells.'

'It'll be far enough, my lad, for us to be caught up in fog, or skid off the road, or have to be dug out of drifts. Oh no, you're not getting me going up there this time of the year. Anyway, they tell you on the telly not to go along those roads unless you must.'

'I'll go by train then,' said Joe flatly.

'That's up to you,' said his father, sitting down again.

Looking at his mother now Joe said, 'I'll have to leave on Saturday; I'll stay overnight if they'll have me.'

'Who's going to look after that horse?' said his father now.

'Anna will.'

'You're lucky to have that lass,' said Mr Darling;

111

'It isn't every girl that'd spend her time in stables mucking about after an old bone-shaker.'

'He's not a bone-shaker, Dad.'

'Joe! mind your tone.' It was his mother again, and Joe looked at her and walked out of the room and into his own, banging the door behind him.

Mrs Darling now looked at her husband, then said quietly, 'I wouldn't mind a run out on Sunday if it's fine.'

'Aw you,' said Mr Darling.

'Well, it might solve the problem if they take the horse.'

'There's only one problem that'll ever solve that horse,' said Mr Darling, 'and you know it and I know it, and he knows it in his heart.' He nodded towards the bedroom door.

'Let me tell him we'll take him, weather permitting,' said Mrs Darling under her breath, and to this Mr Darling merely jerked his chin upwards, then said, 'Before you go and break the glad tidings pour me out another cup of tea.'

# *Nine*

'We're not far off now,' said Joe, looking out of the car window. 'There's only Allendale and Whitfield and we turn off past there.'

'Thank the Lord for that,' said Mr Darling.

When they passed Whitfield and came to the turning off the main road, Mrs Darling asked, 'Is it very far up here?' and Joe, keeping his gaze straight ahead, said, 'Not very, but . . . but it's a bit bumpy and . . . and when you come to this bend along here don't look down.'

'What for?' asked his mother, her voice high now.

'Well, you don't like heights do you, so don't look down.'

'I needn't be told twice about that,' said Mrs Darling, but when they rounded the bend she did look down and she gasped when from the narrow road she saw the hillside dropping sheer to the valley below.

Even Mr Darling, glancing sideways, remarked under his breath, 'That's a drop! Why don't they rail it round? You could go over there if you didn't know anything about it.'

The car was running downhill now, bumping and jolting over holes and ruts, and Joe tried to close his ears to his father's pithy comments. Then they ran into the familiar piece of woodland, not black dark like it had been in the summer time when the trees were thick with leaves, but nevertheless dim enough to make Mrs Darling exclaim, 'Now, where are we going?'

'We're nearly there,' said Joe; 'Once we get through you'll see it. There!' He pointed excitedly. 'There's the farm. Eeh! it's as if I'd never been away. Look! look, there's Matty and Jessica.'

'Sit down. Sit down,' said Mr Darling.

A minute or so later Joe was out of the car and shaking Matty's two hands up and down; then saying to Jessica 'Hello there, Jessica. How are you?' and Jessica saying, 'Oh, I'm fine, Joe. It's nice to see you, Joe.'

'Thanks,' said Joe. 'This is me mam and dad.'

The introductions over, Mr Darling looked at Matty and said, 'Man, you've grown; I wouldn't have recognized you if I'd met you in the street.'

'You're liking it, Matty?' asked Mrs Darling, and Matty said, 'Nothing ever better. It's the life.'

Mr Darling was now looking about him and he remarked under his breath, 'The life? Aye, it might be for some.'

From the minute his dad and Mr Walsh met, Joe was filled with a feeling of apprehension, they didn't hit it off. His dad, he knew, was a man who could get on with most people, and Mr Walsh, he also knew, was a man who it was very difficult to get to know. His manner was brusque and down to earth and he didn't seem to mind what he said or whom he offended. Yet beneath it all he was a kind, good man. Joe had had proof of this during their short acquaintance; and look what he had done for Matty.

Joe became lost in a deepening hopelessness during the meal as he heard Mr Walsh counter everything his dad said. His mother, too, he knew, had sensed the feeling between the two men, but Mrs Walsh didn't seem affected by it. She laughed and chatted and pressed second helpings on them all and told them how much she enjoyed having Matty on the farm and what a good boy he was, and then she related for the benefit of her guests all the incidents that had taken place during the camping session, and Mr Walsh butted in towards the end of the story, saying, 'Yes, they were a lot of greenhorns all right. When I saw them standing in the station yard that day I thought they looked as if they had just been dug up.'

'That could apply both ways,' said Mr Darling now. And Joe shivered inside. He didn't really blame his dad, because Mr Walsh was getting him on the raw. But oh, oh how he wished he had come on his own.

After the meal was over, Mr Walsh, in his brusque way, rose from the table, saying. 'Well now, we'll have to get down to this business, won't we, because you'll want to get back while the light's good?'

It was almost like pushing them out of the door and Joe daren't look at his parents, but he cast a glance towards Matty, and Matty grinned back at him reassuringly, the grin, saying, Well, you know Mr Walsh.

In the comfortable sitting-room Mr Walsh

pointed out the seating to them; then dropping into a big leather chair to the side of the roaring fire, he lit his pipe before addressing Joe pointedly, saying, 'Well, down to facts. Let's have them.'

'W . . . Well, it's like this, Mr Walsh.' Joe began hesitantly. 'This horse I've been left, he's a sort of nice beast, and I don't want him to be put down, but . . . but I can't see me way to doing it on me pocket money.'

'What is your pocket money?'

'Fifteen shillings.'

'You're lucky.' The words were clipped. 'But even so that amount won't feed and stable a horse.'

'No, Mr Walsh, that's it.'

'So what do you want me to do about it?'

'Well, you see I could manage to pay for his feed. Me mam here says, she'll go five shillings.'

'And you can count me in an' all.' It was his father, his voice high and defiant now. 'We don't want charity for the horse, or anything else.'

As Joe bowed his head Mr Walsh jerked his chin up, saying. 'I'm glad to hear that, oh, I'm glad to hear that.' Then turning his attention to Joe again, he went on, 'You know what it costs to keep a horse, taking it all round, you can't do it on a pound a week.'

'I know,' said Joe.

'Well, that means you'd be without pocket money; how do you feel about that?'

'I'll get a rise next year.'

'A year's a long time to go without pocket money.'

'I'll . . . I'll manage as long as the horse is all right.'

'They call it The Gladiator, I understand.'

116

There was no laughter on Mr Walsh's face and Joe, looking straight back at him, said, 'Aye, that's his name, The Gladiator.'

'Does he look like one?'

'No, not my idea of a gladiator; he's old and bony. I might as well tell you, folks laugh at him.' Joe was sticking to the truth; the whole situation was hopeless and there was nothing to be lost by it, but he added, 'Them that have got nothing better to laugh at that is.'

'And there are a good many of them about,' commented Mr Walsh sagely.

There was a silence following this; then Mr Walsh said, 'Well, now, I don't rightly know. Apart from his feeding – we won't talk about his stabling – but apart from his feeding he's got to be looked after. An old horse needs to be looked after.'

'But, Dad, I can see to him when I see to . . .'

'You hold your tongue, young lady.' Mr Walsh nodded towards his daughter. 'What with your schooling, and looking after your pony you've got your hands full already. What would have to be done for this horse would have to be done in somebody's free time.' Mr Walsh did not look towards Matty, but Matty looked towards him and said, 'I'll take it on, Mr Walsh, sort of be responsible for him if you like . . . and in me free time.'

'And it will be in your free time mind,' Mr Walsh nodded sternly towards Matty. Then looking at Joe, who, during the last few moments had become filled with an excitement bred of hope, he said, 'Well, it's nearly all settled then, that is at a pound a week. That's what I'll have to charge, and I'll be out of pocket a bit.'

'Oh, dear, dear,' said Mrs Walsh coming into the room with a tray of tea.

'What did you say?' said her husband.

'Nothing,' said Mrs Walsh. 'Nothing.'

But they all knew that she had clicked her tongue at her husband.

Joe was on his feet now standing to the side of Mr Walsh's chair and, his voice low and filled with emotion, he said, 'I'm more than grateful, Mr Walsh; I don't know how to thank you.'

'Thanking me for robbing you of your pocket money?'

'Oh, you're not doing that, you're doing me a favour, me and The Gladiator. I'll be quite happy when I know he's up here, an' I'll send the money regular.'

'I'll see you do or I'll pack him back to you.'

Again Mrs Walsh made a sound, and again her husband said, 'What's that you say?' And on this both Jessica and Matty burst out laughing.

Joe looked at his one-time friend in surprise. Matty hadn't been the one to laugh easily but now his manner was different; Mr Walsh mustn't be so bad to work for as all that.

The farmer brought Joe's attention to him again by saying, 'There's one thing that everybody seems to have passed over, how are you going to get the animal here? Do you propose walking him?'

Joe laughed gently, then said, 'You can get boxes, can't you?'

'Yes, yes.' Mr Walsh nodded. 'You can get boxes, but boxes cost money. Have you any idea what it would cost to bring a horse box from Shields up here?'

'No,' said Joe.

'Well, it's only a matter of fifty miles I grant you, and a car could do it in a couple of hours, rough road an' all, but when you've got livestock behind you, you don't gallop so to speak. I reckon it would be the best part of a day for a man, and that is if the weather holds and he gets straight through. It's my guess that it'll cost you on the far side of ten pounds.'

'Ten pounds!' Joe's voice spiralled high into his head.

'I could pull a trailer behind my car,' put in Mr Darling now, only to be almost shouted down by Mr Walsh, saying, 'Don't be absurd, man.'

Mr Darling was sitting on the edge of his chair. 'I'm not absurd, thank you, I've pulled a caravan afore the day.'

'You may have,' said Mr Walsh calmly; 'granted you may have, but horse boxes are a different thing; they are specialized, made to carry animals, and the drivers are generally used to driving them.'

Joe's heart sank when he saw his father look abruptly at his watch, then say grimly, 'Time's getting on, Mona.'

'Yes,' said Mrs Darling; 'but I would like to have looked round the farm.' Her voice was placatory as she glanced towards Mr Walsh, and he, smiling at her and getting to his feet, said, 'No sooner said than done, madam; it'll be a pleasure.'

Mrs Darling did not look at her husband but sidled to her feet and followed Mr Walsh from the room.

When Mrs Walsh too had left the room, Joe, looking at his father, said pleadingly, 'Don't spoil it, Dad.'

'Now look here, Joe . . .'

'All right, all right, Dad, I know how you feel, but wait till we get home.'

Mr Darling drew in a long breath, then settled back deeply in his chair.

Jessica, now looking at Matty, said, 'Aren't you going to show Joe round? I'll stay with Mr Darling.' She smiled at the scowling man and Matty, getting to his feet, grinned at Joe saying, 'Come on. You've seen it all afore, but come on.'

Mrs Walsh was in the kitchen as they passed through and she put her hand on Joe's arm and smiling down into his face, she whispered, 'It's going to be all right; don't worry about them. Mr Walsh likes to have the upper hand. Don't you remember?' Her smile widened. 'It's his way. He'd have the horse here if it was only to have your father beholden to him.' She chuckled; then her voice dropping to a whisper, she said, 'They didn't take to each other. It very often happens with men, as with women.'

Joe suddenly felt at peace, he felt as if the weight had been completely lifted from his shoulders, and he smiled back at Mrs Walsh but didn't speak. There was no need for words from him; she was a very wise woman was Mrs Walsh, very wise.

But when they got into the yard Joe said, 'She's nice, isn't she?'

'She's marvellous,' said Matty; 'but mind—' he turned and thumbed Joe with the old mannerism – 'don't you go calling on me mam when you get back and telling her that I think Mrs Walsh is marvellous. She's jealous enough of her already.'

'Women!' said Joe on a high laugh now.

'Aye, and men an' all,' added Matty knowingly.

'If ever I met a pig of a man he's one,' said Mr Darling before his wife and Joe had finished waving to the Walsh family and Matty. 'If I never clap eyes on him again that'll be one time too many.'

'I found him all right,' said Mrs Darling; 'It was how you handled him.'

'Handled him? He started on me from the word go; you'd think I'd done something to the man.'

'He's like that, Dad,' said Joe quietly. 'When we first met him, we couldn't stand him. He was ordering us about all over the place, but after a while we found it was just his manner. He's all right underneath.'

'Well, I won't bother digging,' said Mr Darling. 'As for him taking the animal, you'd think you weren't paying for him, the condescension was oozing out of him. I bet it doesn't take a pound a week to keep a horse there, he'll get everything wholesale, and one thing goes in with another on a farm. Oh, you can't tell me. He's not the man to do anything for nothing, he'll be making on the side. And when I'm on, where do you think you're going to get ten pounds to bring the horse here? I'm not going to lend you ten pounds.'

'I didn't ask you, Dad.'

'Well, who are you going to ask?'

'That's my business.'

'You start getting into debt at your age and you'll never get out ... That old fellow should have been shot for leaving you the animal. I know, if I had my way, what I would do the minute I get back.'

'Well, you haven't got your way,' said Mrs Darling quietly, 'so let's forget it. And look we're coming to that big drop and unless you want to put an end to all our troubles keep your eyes on the road.'

'Hand me my bag there,' said Mrs Darling, now turning round to Joe, and as he gave her her handbag she winked at him and the wink told him not to worry about the transport, he could rely on her help, and he winked back to her.

The Gladiator was settled; he was fixed for the remainder of his life; everything was wonderful. He felt so happy he could sing.

# *Ten*

Yes, everything was wonderful but the weather.

Mr Billings had arranged for a horse box for The Gladiator. Whether he had put any money out of his own pocket towards the cost Joe didn't know, but he strongly suspected that must be the case, because Mr Billings said the man was only going to charge six pounds. The Gladiator was going to his new home on Saturday.

Joe knew he was going to miss The Gladiator more than anything or anybody who had been in his life before. He told him this on the Thursday night as he stroked his muzzle. 'I'm going to miss you, boy,' he said; 'but you'll like it there, you'll like Matty, and in the spring you'll have piles of grass and places to roam in; you'll have a new lease of life, man. But still—' he paused – 'I'm going to miss you.'

But after all Joe wasn't going to lose The Gladiator so soon, for during Thursday night it started to snow and it snowed all day on the Friday and on the Saturday too, and the driver called in on the Saturday morning and said, 'It's no use. I couldn't get through in this; we might get stuck some place and it wouldn't be fair on him.' And he nodded at The

Gladiator. And Joe said, 'Well, when can you do it?'

The driver consulted a well-thumbed book and said, 'Next Wednesday afternoon, or Saturday, if it's clear by then.'

'We'll just have to wait then,' said Joe, 'won't we?'

'Can't be helped,' said the driver.

'No,' said Joe.

'I'll call in and tell Mr Billings,' said the driver.

The driver hadn't been gone more than ten minutes when the stable door opened again. Joe turned, thinking it was Anna, but it wasn't, it was the man, the nosey man, the man called Tellman.

'Hello,' said the man, closing the stable door behind him.

'Hello,' said Joe, staring at him.

'I . . . I understand you're letting the horse go,' said the man.

'Aye,' said Joe. 'He was going the day but the fellow can't take him because of the roads.'

The man now looked down at his feet; then looked at Joe and, his voice low, he said, 'I . . . I want to give you a bit of advice. Don't let the horse go at all.'

'What are you talking about?'

'Just what I say. I . . . I would hang on to him if I were you. I wouldn't let him go.'

'But it's for his own good.'

'It . . . it might be, but . . . but I'd keep him for a time if I were you.'

'Who are you, mister?'

'My name is Tellman. I told you.'

'You something to do with the R.S.P.C.A.?'

'Oh no, no, nothing.'

'The P.D.S.A. then?'

'No, no, nor the P.D.S.A.'

Joe thought hard, and then he felt he had got it. 'The Anti-vivisection thing, that's what you're about, isn't it? You think I'm sending him to one of those labs; well, I'm not . . . Coo! Lor! what do you think I am?'

'No, no,' said Mr Tellman, shaking his head. 'Nothing like that.'

'Well, what are you after then?' said Joe.

'Nothing, nothing; I'm just interested in you and the horse.'

'What for?' asked Joe pointedly now.

'What for?' said the man. 'Well—' he looked down at his shoes – 'only because I think it was very good of you to look after the horse, and I think that you should go on looking after him.'

'You're talking through your hat,' said Joe; 'you don't know what it's like. And then me money's running out. I've got him on a nice farm, he'll be all right.'

At this point the door opened again and Anna entered, and the man said. 'Well . . . well, I'll be going, but if I were you I'd take my advice: hang on to him for a bit.'

'Who's he?' asked Anna.

'You're asking me. This is the fourth time he's been here. He said I shouldn't send The Gladiator to the farm, I should keep him here.'

'He's a crank,' said Anna. 'There's lots of them about where animals are concerned. Daddy has to deal with them all the time. He had one last week. There was a cat. It was knocked down and its inside was nearly out—' she hunched her shoulders up round her face and bit tightly on her lip – 'but the owner wouldn't let daddy put it to sleep, not at first. She said she could heal it herself by putting her hands on it. The only good thing, as daddy said, was that the poor animal was so far gone it was unconscious. There are lots of cranks like that.' She paused a minute, then added, 'Isn't it awful, this snow? I could cry. Poor, poor Gladiator.' She went up to the horse and put her arms around its neck; then, turning to Joe, she said, 'Yet at the same time I'm glad he's here for a little while longer. I'm going to miss him, aren't you, Joe?'

Joe didn't answer; he was thinking of the man. There was something fishy about him. An awful thought entering his mind, he turned to Anna and whispered, 'Look, that fellow; do you think he's planning to steal him and sell him? You know some people will do anything for money. They all say he would bring a good few pounds in the knacker's yard. Perhaps that's why he's telling me I should hang on to him; perhaps he had planned to pinch him.'

'Yes,' said Anna, looking suddenly serious, 'you're probably right. He did look shifty. You'd better lock up well tonight.'

'You'll bet I'll lock up well. And I'll do more than that. I'll sleep here till he goes. Oh—' he rubbed The Gladiator's nose softly – 'I'd go round the bend if something happened to him now.'

'I'd go round the bend with you,' endorsed Anna; then she added. 'Do you mean it about sleeping here?'

126

'Course I do,' said Joe. 'It'll be no use closing the stable door after the horse is stolen, will it?'

'No, I suppose not,' said Anna.

'Boy, you're stark staring mad,' said Mrs Darling, 'sleeping in that place all by yourself. Oh! that horse. Why can't you get rid of him?'

'I would have been rid of him, as you call it, if it wasn't for the snow.'

'And you'll get rid of yourself before you get rid of him if you go sleeping in that ice-box in this weather.'

'It's not really cold in there, Mam. With the straw and the heat from his body it even gets fuggy. An' I've got me camping-out kit.'

'Be quiet!' said Mrs Darling. 'I won't listen to you, I'll let your dad deal with you . . .'

And Mr Darling did deal with Joe. He dealt with him in a very surprising way, at least surprising to his wife. He said, 'Good idea, as long as you keep warm. And why not ask Willie to kip along with you?'

'Not on your life!' said Joe. 'He'd take more looking after than the burglars.'

'And how do you intend to cope with horse thieves if they do show up?' his mother asked scathingly.

'Yell the place down,' said Joe. 'That's all.'

'You're mad,' said his mother. 'And he's worse than you.' She now glared at her husband. But Mr Darling and Joe smiled at each other.

It had all sounded easy, sleeping in the stable with The Gladiator. But now, at twelve o'clock at night, lying wide-eyed staring into the blackness,

127

it was frightening. Joe wasn't cold, he was well tucked down in his sleeping bag on a thick layer of straw. He'd just finished half-a-thermos flask of soup and his stomach should have been feeling warm and soothed; instead it was trembling like a cold jelly.

It was very quiet in the stable. There was nothing but the sound of The Gladiator's heavy breathing. He strained his ears to hear the sound of a car passing, but there was nothing; nothing, until about half an hour later the footsteps came up the yard.

He must have been almost dozing, but now he was sitting bolt upright, his body stiff. When the latch of the stable door was lifted he opened his mouth to shout, but it remained agape as a voice said, 'Police here. You all right in there, young 'un?'

Like a pricked balloon his body folded up and he called back, 'Yes, thanks.'

'Look back later,' said the voice, and again he said, 'Thanks.'

His dad had done it after all. He said he would look in at the police station and tell them when he came out of the club. Coo, Lord! he was sweating. He smiled to himself now, and when The Gladiator neighed softly, he said to him, 'I'll never be more frightened than I was just now, so why worry.'

And on this he lay down and went to sleep; and when his alarm clock went off at six o'clock he woke up and groaned, 'Oh lor! why do I do it? I must be barmy.'

And those were the words his mother said to him when, at seven o'clock, after having seen to

The Gladiator, he reached home. 'Why do you do it, boy? You must be barmy.'

It didn't thaw by Wednesday, and Joe was still sleeping in the stable. He felt he had been sleeping there all his life and would go on sleeping there for the remainder of it.

When Mr Billings heard about the man and what Joe thought he intended to do, he said, 'Well, it was just possible.' And this didn't make Joe any happier.

Then, on account of the weather he had to pay for another week's stabling, and this meant he hadn't enough money for the usual amount of seed hay.

When another week actually passed and the ground was still icy things really became desperate.

When Anna proffered, 'You can have all my pocket money,' Joe said, 'Thanks all the same but . . . but it won't be enough. It's the stabling, you see. I'll have to ask me dad.'

To Joe's surprise his dad didn't go off the deep-end. 'How much do you want?' he said.

'A pound will see me over,' said Joe; 'This weather can't last for ever.'

'You'd be surprised,' said his father.

The thaw set in on the Wednesday, and there was every indication of the roads being clear by the Saturday. Joe went round to see the driver and the man said, Yes, Saturday would be all right, weather providing, and would he like to come along with him for company?

Oh, aye. Yes, Joe said; he would love that for then he would be able to see The Gladiator settled in.

Then on the Friday night, the last night The

Gladiator was to spend in his old home, the man came again, and the sight of him nearly frightened the wits out of Joe. The man stood within the stable door looking at Joe. 'He's still here then?' he said.

'Aye,' said Joe gruffly. 'You surprised?'

'In a way yes; and in another way no.'

'That's as clear as mud,' said Joe.

When the man laughed softly Joe said, 'Look here, who are you anyway? Are you connected with animals in any way?'

'No, I wouldn't say that.'

'Well, what do you work at?' demanded Joe now.

'I work in an office.'

Joe was puzzled. 'An office?' he said. 'Did you know The Gladiator afore I had him then? Is that why you're interested?'

'I've seen him around,' said the man; 'but who in Shields hasn't?'

Joe let this pass. 'If you've no connection with animals and you just work in an office what interest have you in him?' Joe asked pointedly.

'None at all really,' said the man.

'No interest?' said Joe, his voice rising. 'Then what brings you round here?' He almost added, 'Scaring the wits out of me.'

'You,' said the man.

'Me?' Joe dug his fingers into his chest. 'You interested in me? What for?' His tone was aggressive now.

'Oh, well.' The man dropped his head toward his shoulders. 'Let's say because I think you're a very kind boy to take such an interest in a creature such as him.'

'I don't get it,' said Joe.

'It's as clear as mud,' said the man using Joe's

own words, and Joe nodded, saying, 'Aye, you could say that again. Anyway,' he added, 'the night's the last night, he'll be gone the morrow, and there won't be any need for you to come . . . come round after this.' He only just stopped himself from inserting snooping, and went on. 'Anyway, the place will be shut up, I'm not paying any more rent.'

'No, you'll be well in pocket,' said the man.

'What do you mean?' asked Joe.

'Well—' the man inclined his head before going on, 'I understand you're selling him to a farmer and then you'll be saved the cost of his feeding . . .'

'Well, you understand wrong, you see. Whoever informed you of that, they gave you the wrong story. I'm not selling him to a farmer, I'm putting him out on a farm and paying for him.'

The man's eyebrows went up, his mouth opened a little and then he said, 'Oh, you are? Oh, I have been misinformed. I understood you had sold him. Not that it makes any difference now, you understand?'

'No, I don't understand; I'm all at sea with you,' said Joe.

At this the man laughed out loud; then he said quietly, 'Well, always remember, Mr Darling, that it's a very wide ocean that hasn't a port. Good night.'

Joe looked at the closed door. Mr Darling he had called him. And it's a very wide ocean that hasn't a port, just because he had said he was all at sea. He was an odd bloke, cranky. Eeh! there were some funny folks about. In a way he was glad he wouldn't be seeing him again, there was

131

something very fishy about him. Aye, something very fishy.

And he said so to Mr Billings when, some-time later, he went around to the house to ask if Anna had got permission to accompany them tomorrow.

'Yes, he does sound fishy, to say the least,' said Mr Billings. 'I've made a few enquiries about him, but there's no one of that name connected with the animal societies in the town.'

'No, he said he wasn't. I asked him. He said he worked in an office.'

'In an office? How old is he?'

'Oh, round sixty I should say.'

Mr Billings looked away and he thought for a moment; then he said, 'Well, you show him the gate when he comes again, Joe. If he can't state what his business is, tell him to get going.'

'But I won't be there, Mr Billings.'

'Oh, of course, you won't. But you never know. If he seeks you out tell him you'll put the police on him. That should settle him.'

'I will, Mr Billings.'

'In the meantime I'll make more enquiries about him ... Now about tomorrow. I under-stand you're leaving about half past ten, so you should get there about one. That's taking it easy, and Grant is a careful driver. I'll see him in the morning before he leaves and tell him I want you back here before dark because although the roads are clear at present, snow or fog can strike like lightning up on those fells. What we've got to do tonight is to pray that we won't have any rain and then a frost, and that the sun will shine tomorrow.'

'Yes, Mr Billings.' Joe wanted to say that he heartily endorsed the substance of this prayer, but what he did say was, 'I'll work overtime on it,' and they both laughed.

And the following morning it was as if the prayer had been answered. The air was mild and the sun was shining. Joe had got up early, brushed The Gladiator well down and got him ready for the road, then had gone home, had his breakfast and changed into his good things. And now here he was standing alone with The Gladiator waiting for the van to arrive. He had his two hands on the animal's cheeks and, his voice holding a cracked sound, he said, 'You'll have your fling up there, lad, an' I hope it makes up for all the years of hard graft and being stuck in this place, 'cos in spite of having Mr Prodhurst, it's been no fun. But mind—' he tapped the horse's nostril – 'don't you forget I'm still your boss. Don't you go and take such a fancy to Matty that when I come along you won't even remember me. Now mind, I'm telling you.'

The Gladiator now tossed his head and let out a loud neigh, but Joe couldn't laugh at it. There was a tightness in his throat and a burning in his eyes and he had to turn away, and scrub his face wildly with his handkerchief as he heard the back gate open and Anna came running up the yard, calling, 'The van's here, Joe.'

Mr Billings had come too and he admired Joe's handiwork on The Gladiator. He looked at the horse as Anna stood caressing him, and he said, 'Well, your private war's all but over, Joe.'

Private war, he called it, thought Joe. Well, he

supposed it had been a kind of war against everybody who had wanted him to have The Gladiator put down. Joe smiled at the vet and said, 'I suppose you could say that, Mr Billings.'

'You'll be sorry to lose him even with all the trouble he's caused you?'

'Yes, I will, Mr Billings.'

'Apparently you're not the only one, I understand someone arrived home in . . .'

'Father!' cried Anna.

'Well, it's no disgrace,' said Mr Billings. 'If you can't cry over an animal you won't cry over a human being.'

'Are we ready?' said Sam Grant, coming into the stable, and Mr Billings looked at Joe, and Joe said, 'Aye.'

The Gladiator needed a great deal of persuasion to mount the ramp and enter the strange stall. Three times he jumped off the side and into the road. Then Joe went into the box and coaxed him, saying, 'Come on, come on, boy. I'll stay with you,' and The Gladiator, after looking steadfastly at Joe for a moment, went slowly towards him.

'Stay with him for a while,' said Mr Billings, 'until he quietens down. There's not all that hurry. Perhaps it would be as well if you stayed in the box with him.'

'Won't he trample on me if he gets terrified?' said Joe.

'It's a point,' laughed Mr Billings.

'He'll be all right,' said Sam Grant, fastening The Gladiator's halter securely, then shutting up the drop door. 'They get used to the rhythm after a time. Get up front and talk to him, let him know you're there.'

'Up you both get,' said Mr Billings now, helping Anna into the cab, and addressing Sam Grant he said, 'And mind what I said, Sam. Don't let them stay and watch the animal going mad with freedom. Time flies; get them back here before dark if you can.'

'Will do,' said Sam.

The moment the engine started and the van moved slowly forward The Gladiator let out a loud piercing neigh and Joe shouted at the top of his voice, 'It's all right! It's all right, boy, I'm here.'

And for the next two or three miles he kept calling to The Gladiator, who neighed in reply, and Sam Grant remarked, 'It's a talking horse you've got there all right.'

After a while a silence enveloped them and Joe remarked to no one in particular, 'It's a lovely day,' and Anna said, 'Yes, it is a lovely day.' And Sam Grant said, 'While it lasts.' They then all lapsed into silence again.

'Do you want to stop for a hot drink or something?' asked Sam after they had been going for about an hour, and Joe looked at Anna and when she shook her head he said, 'I'm all right; I had a big breakfast.'

'Well, the less time we waste the quicker we'll get there,' said Sam. And on they went.

The last part of the journey was the worst, as Joe knew it would be. The rutted road and the steep sloping hillside caused Sam to say, 'You're sure we're still in England, not up the Alps or somewhere? We're nearly there you say?'

'Yes, a few more minutes now. Through this woodland, and then you'll see it.'

And then they were there. And it would appear that the entire Walsh family was awaiting them, for on the road were Mr Walsh, Matty and Jessica and hurrying from the house was Mrs Walsh.

'Well, you've made it.' Mr Walsh held up his arms and lifted Anna to the ground, then said, 'Hello, young lady.'

'Hello, Sir,' said Anna.

'My daughter,' said Mr Walsh, making abrupt introductions; 'and that's Matty. And here's my wife.' And without pausing he went on, addressing Joe now, 'And now young fellow, journey's end and all that?'

'Yes, Mr Walsh.'

'Think he'll still be alive?'

'I hope so, Mr Walsh.' Joe gave a nervous laugh and he had a renewed feeling of apprehension concerning how Mr Walsh would react when he saw The Gladiator.

When the ramp was let down The Gladiator made no attempt to emerge. He seemed a little dazed, and Joe, going up to him, said softly, 'Come on, boy. Come on. You're home.'

The Gladiator was now standing on the roadway and the Walsh family and Matty were staring at him, and nobody laughed. Whether they had arranged among themselves that they weren't going to laugh at the horse no matter what it looked like, or they were so filled with compassion at the sight of the bony old creature that laughter would have been a form of blasphemy, Joe didn't know. He only knew that he was grateful to them for their reaction.

Jessica was the first to move towards the

horse. Touching his muzzle she said, 'Hello, old boy.' For answer The Gladiator tossed his head once, then slowly moved it from side to side; then his nostrils widened and quivered, and he turned completely about and looked towards the field where Joe, Matty and Willie had camped last year, and Mrs Walsh exclaimed, 'Well, I never! He's scented Ladybird.'

'He has an' all,' said Mr Walsh.

'It's my pony,' said Jessica to Anna. 'We brought her out just a little while ago, she's at the bottom of the field.' She ran now with Anna by her side to the gate and, climbing on it, stuck two fingers in her mouth and gave a whistle as shrill as any boy could.

The pony came racing up the field and by the time it reached the gate they were all there, with The Gladiator to the fore.

The Gladiator looked over the gate at the cob, then it startled the entire company, the imperturbable Mr Walsh included, by letting out the most terrific neigh.

'Open the gate, open the gate!' Mr Walsh cried, and when Matty pulled the gate wide there was no need to lead The Gladiator through.

When Jessica, followed by Anna and the boys, made a move as if to enter the field Mr Walsh ordered, 'Come out and leave them alone. All of you, come on.'

And now they stood and watched the meeting. Joe, with his hands gripping the crossbar of the gate, watched the quiver pass over the smooth brown coat of the young horse as The Gladiator's head came down to her. He watched the two muzzles remain still for a moment, and then The

Gladiator took a step forward and rubbed his head against the other's neck; and the young horse, after a seeming moment of hesitation, returned the compliment by gently pushing its nose under The Gladiator's uneven mane. This went on for some minutes. Then, as if animated by a spring, the young horse seemed to lift itself from the ground, all four feet together, and was away galloping like a deer across the field.

For a second The Gladiator watched her; then he trotted after her. But only for the first dozen yards or so, for, as if he had been prodded in the hind quarters with a spear, he was galloping, galloping after Ladybird.

'He's running! He's running! Galloping! Look at him! Look at him!'

They were all yelling now, encouraging The Gladiator on as if he were in a race.

'Well I never!' cried Mr Walsh. 'If anybody had asked me my opinion five minutes ago I would have said flatly he hadn't a trot in him. But just look at him.'

'He's caught her up. He's caught her up. Look.' Joe was hanging over the top bar of the gate now, the girls and Matty on one side, the grown-ups on the other, and as the two horses came racing up the sloping field side by side the sound of their galloping was drowned by the cheers. And Joe's was loudest of all. Then they all doubled up with laughter when The Gladiator, stopping suddenly and after standing panting for a moment, lowered his angular body down to the ground and rolled over.

'I think they've had enough now,' said Mr Walsh finally, wiping his eyes. 'Go and fetch them in. He'll have to get used to his new quarters, though by the look of things I don't think that'll be much trouble to him.'

Ten minutes later they'd introduced The Gladiator to his stable and as soon as they closed the half-door on him he came and put his head over it, neighing softly now, and Sam Grant laughed, saying. 'The old boy's got it bad; he wants to know where she is.' And when Ladybird poked her head from her box The Gladiator was satisfied.

'I often wondered what I would do with that other stable,' said Mr Walsh. 'Time and time again I've been going to break the wall down and add it on to the byres, but there, it hadn't to be.'

'Come on all of you,' said Mrs Walsh, 'and have something to eat. They've had enough excitement for the time being; let him settle down . . . let them both settle down. She's as excited as he is.'

The dinner was a merry affair, and following it, just before they took their leave, Joe said quietly to Mr Walsh, 'Can I have a word with you for a minute, Sir?'

'Yes, yes, boy.' Mr Walsh led the way into his office and there, seating himself on the corner of a paper-strewn desk, he said, 'Well, what is it?'

'I just want to thank you, Mr Walsh, for what you're doing. And I hope you're not going to be offended at what I'm going to say.' When he paused Mr Walsh said, 'Well I won't know about that until you say it, will I?'

'No, Sir. Well, it's just this. I still want The Gladiator to belong to me, do you mind?'

'Mind?' Mr Walsh stood up. 'You're paying for him, aren't you?'

'Aye, I know, but I feel I'm not payin' as much

as I should. It's only that I want to feel that he's ... well ...'

Mr Walsh now put his hand on Joe's shoulder and, his voice quiet and deep, he said, 'You've got no need to say any more, boy. I know how you feel. The horse is yours and nobody else's; we're stabling him for you.'

'Oh thanks, Mr Walsh. I'm glad you don't mind.'

'Now why should I mind about that? This was a business deal.'

'Aye,' said Joe on a laugh. 'Business deal. But I feel I'm getting the best of the bargain.'

'Well, it's a nice feeling, isn't it, getting the best of a bargain? I enjoy it at times myself. Go on and get yourselves off. I want to know you've reached home safe; the weather's unpredictable up here, more so at this time of the year. One more thing.' He halted Joe as he was going out of the door. 'You're welcome to come here any time you like.'

'Oh thank you, Mr Walsh! You're very good.'

Mr Walsh's answer to this was to give Joe a push between the shoulder blades that sent him out into the kitchen again where the others were waiting, and Jessica, in her perky way, said, 'Is he braying you?'

'Aye,' said Joe on a laugh. 'He knocked me about something awful.'

They were all moving out into the farmyard when Anna stopped and, looking back into the large comfortable farm kitchen, suddenly exclaimed, 'Oh, I do wish I were staying here.'

'You do, dear?' said Mrs Walsh on a pleased note.

'Yes. The farm and everything's marvellous. The hills and the air. Oh, the whole place is wonderful.'

'Well, you'll have to come for a holiday,' said Jessica.

'Could I?'

'Why not?' said Mrs Walsh. 'Why not indeed! And Joe an' all.'

'What's that?' said Joe.

'They're arranging for you to come for your holidays,' said Matty, nudging him.

'Oh,' said Joe. 'Yes, that would be nice.' But his tone did not express much pleasure at the prospect. He would like a holiday up here with Matty and The Gladiator, but having two lasses around, well, he didn't know how that would work out, but still, as girls went they weren't too bad. There was one thing in their favour, they had more things in their heads than twisting.

At the last moment, as Joe went in the direction of The Gladiator's box and Anna made to follow, Mr Walsh put his hand gently on her arm and when she looked at him he shook his head.

Joe opened the door and went into the stable. The Gladiator was contentedly munching hay but lifted his head, then stepped towards Joe. And Joe put his arms about him, at least as much of him as they would encompass, and he bit tight down on his lip for a moment before saying, 'So long, old fellow. So long. I'll be back. Enjoy yourself.'

The Gladiator now made a small sound that told Joe he understood, and when Joe left the box the horse came to the door and, putting his head over, he neighed loudly. But Joe didn't look back.

All he wanted to do now was to get away as quickly as possible in case he had to bring his hankie out.

When they were seated in the cab of the lorry Matty got up on the step and said quietly to Joe, 'Don't worry about a thing. I'll see to him. And I think he's in for the happiest days of his life.'

'Thanks, Matty.' It was all Joe could say, and then they were off, and no one spoke, not even Sam Grant, not even when they crossed the road above the big drop; in fact the whole journey back to Shields was uninteresting. It didn't snow; they didn't run into sleet or fog; it was notable only for its lack of conversation. But just before they reached the town Sam Grant said, 'I've carted many animals in me time but that old horse had something, he got you somehow.'

And deep in his heart Joe endorsed that. The Gladiator got you somehow.

# Eleven

Sunday was the dreariest day Joe had experienced in a long time. He sat about the house; he looked at the television; he went for a walk; and then he sat about the house again and looked at the television. As his father pointed out, days were longer when you hadn't any money in your pocket, and he had saddled himself with something for years ahead, for the horse as old as it was, could live in its present environment until it was twenty-five or more.

So Monday morning, for once, was welcome to Joe. He even welcomed the sight of Willie, surprisingly waiting for him at the corner of his street as he went to work.

'Hello,' said Willie.

'Hello,' said Joe.

There was one thing about Willie; he never bore you any grudge whatever you said to him. Perhaps it was because his skin was so thick, nothing ever penetrated it.

'Got it all over?' asked Willie now.

'Got what over?' said Joe, although he knew exactly what Willie meant.

'Moving the old boy. You know what I mean.'

'Oh that,' said Joe. 'Yes, he's settled in.'

143

'How did you find Matty?' asked Willie.

'Oh, he's grand, on top of the world.'

'He f . . . fell on his feet in that job,' said Willie. 'I w . . . wish I had taken it.'

'Don't talk so wet, man; you never got the chance of it, you never would. And anyway, you broke your neck to get out of the country, you were terrified of the quiet.'

'No, I wasn't. There you g . . . go again, exaggerating.'

'Me exaggerating! Aw, what does it matter?'

As they turned into the shipyard gates Willie broke the silence by saying, 'Things will be back to normal now, eh?'

'What do you mean by normal?'

'Well, you must admit you've never been the s . . . same since that old horse c . . . came on the scene. And now it's gone, the lass'll be gone an' all.'

'The lass? Anna, you mean?'

'Who else? She's just one of those girls who are horse mad. That's why she came around; it was the horse.'

'Oh ta! Thanks,' said Joe. 'Thanks a lot.'

'Well, ask yourself, man. She goes to the High School.'

'I don't care if she goes to St Trinians.'

'Well, don't go down me throat, I'll have a job c . . . c . . . catching hold of your l . . . legs . . . All right, all right, I was only funnin'. Any rate, it's over.'

'Cut it out, man. What's over? What you talkin' about?'

'Just that you won't be seeing her again and we'll be going round like afore.'

'You've got some hope after giving me the go-by all these weeks.'

'Ah well, you know me, Joe; I'm no good at m . . . m . . . muckin' out horses.'

'Nobody's any good at muckin' out horses but some people do it.'

Willie now remarked nonchalantly, 'I'm thinking of getting a m . . . motor bike.'

'Good for you.'

'I thought we could run out and see Matty now and again, and it would be a cheap way of you seeing the old moke.'

'He's not an old moke,' Joe barked at him now. 'As for a cheap way of getting there, aye, it'll be cheap with me buying the petrol. That's what you're after isn't it? Oh, I know you, Willie Styles.'

'Eeh! You're in a t . . . temper this mornin', aren't you? An' if you did buy the petrol it wouldn't be one quarter what you'd have to pay on the train. But if you're not interested.'

'No. I'm not interested.'

'Hello, Joe,' shouted one man as they boarded the ship. 'Hear you've sold your horse?'

Joe didn't answer; he was amazed how fast news travelled, and he turned to Willie and said, 'You been doin' the town crier's act over the week-end?'

'No. Why p . . . pick on me?'

'What . . . what did you get for him, Joe?' called another man. 'A bag of liquorice allsorts?'

It was during the morning that Harry Farthing came up to him and said quietly, 'They tell me you've got rid of the old fellow?'

Joe found he didn't lose his temper with Harry

145

these days, and so he now answered quietly, 'I haven't got rid of him, Harry, I've put him on a farm.'

'You have? You mean you've still got to pay for him?'

'Aye.'

'How you managing that?'

'Oh, I'm managing, Harry.'

'Well, well, you've got some guts; I'll say that for you, little 'un.' The little 'un brought Joe's stomach muscles tensing, but he made no retort and Harry Farthing went on, 'If you want a sub any time you can call on me. That is up to a Wednesday.' He laughed. 'After that I'm flat broke till Friday night. But I'll be glad to give you a hand out anytime you're stuck, if you get in quick enough.'

Joe looked at the big tousled-haired young man. It was funny how you could hate somebody's guts, then turn to like them. And he was getting to like Harry Farthing, not only because he had been kind to The Gladiator but because he sensed he was good at bottom.

When it neared knocking off time Joe found that he wasn't looking forward to going home because he didn't know what he was going to do with himself. He could catch up on homework, he knew, but that wouldn't fill this lost, empty feeling he had inside. It was as if somebody had died on him, his mam or dad. If he'd had the money he would have got on the phone and asked Mr Walsh how The Gladiator was, but then it would have been a waste because The Gladiator was all right. It was he himself who was all wrong.

If only he could have had a talk with somebody,

Anna say, he would have felt better because next to himself she was the only other person who understood The Gladiator. But, as Willie said, that was finished; he had seen the last of Anna; there was no reason why she should come round anymore. Anyway, there was no place for her to come to. She wouldn't come to their house and he couldn't see himself going to hers.

His mother had just got in a few minutes before him and she was bustling about setting the tea when he entered the kitchen. 'Hello there,' she said; 'how are things?'

He gave her his usual reply. 'All right,' he said.

'There's two letters for you there.' She pointed to the mantelpiece; then drawing him to one side and lowering her voice so it wouldn't reach her husband who was washing himself in the scullery she added, 'You haven't been borrowing from anybody have you?'

'Me borrowing?' he whispered back. 'What would I be borrowing for?'

'That bloomin' horse,' she said. She now poked her face down to his, 'That one—' she thumbed the top letter – 'it's from a solicitor. Look at the back. Peeble & Rice, Fowler Street. Look.'

'Well, I've done nowt. As for borrowing—' he hissed at her – 'I'd have to owe a lot of money to hear from a solicitor.'

'Open it then. Be quick, just in case.' She cast a glance towards the kitchen.

Looking at her disdainfully, Joe now ripped open the envelope and read the brief and formal letter.

'Mr Joseph Darling, 10 Mabel Street, South

Shields, Co. Durham. Dear Sir, I would be obliged if you would call at this office at eleven o'clock on Monday, February 21st. If this time is not suitable to you perhaps you would be kind enough to let me know and make an appointment.

Yours faithfully, James Arthur Peeble.'

Joe looked up at his mother and she looked down at him, and now, as Mr Darling came from the scullery, she turned to her husband and said, 'Look at this. What do you make of it?'

Joe held out the letter to his father, and he watched him read it.

'Know anything about it?' said Mr Darling.

'No.' Joe's voice was high. 'I don't know why they want to see me.'

'It can't be about money or anything,' said Mrs Darling, 'because they always put in "when you will hear something to your advantage", don't they? Like when they are advertising for people in the paper.'

Mr Darling and Joe looked at her; then Joe said, 'Well whatever it is, I can't go the morrow I'm at the college.'

'I would go,' said Mr Darling sitting down at the table.

'You show your master this.' He waved the letter. 'There's something here you've got to find out, one way or another. These solicitors don't send letters out for amusement; they charge about fifteen bob for one the day.'

Now Mrs Darling sat down at the table and, looking at her husband, she said, 'What do you think it can be?'

'Don't ask me, woman. How should I know?'

148

He turned abruptly to his son and demanded. 'You been up to anything on the side?'

'Aw, Dad, you're as bad as mam. Look. What could I get up to on the side, I've spent weeks with The Gladiator? Even if I wanted to or was that way inclined what could I get up to? I haven't had the time.'

'You don't think that Willie Styles has got you incriminated in any way?'

Joe considered this. He wouldn't put it past Willie to mention his name if he got in a jam. But if Willie was in a jam he would have sensed it the day; he couldn't keep anything to himself could Willie. No, he wouldn't know what this was about until tomorrow morning.

'What's the other letter?' asked his mother, interrupting his deductions.

'Oh. Oh that. I don't know. Perhaps from another solicitor.' Joe laughed weakly as he slit open the second letter. Then, his face brightening, he said. 'It's from Anna. They're asking me to tea on Wednesday.'

'Oh, that's nice,' said Mrs Darling. 'Oh, that is nice of her. She's a very nice girl. They're very nice people; you should keep in with them.'

'Aw, Mam.'

Mr Darling endorsed Joe's reaction by jerking his head upwards, and his wife cried at him, 'Well, he should. She's a nice girl, good class an' all that. And mind—' she turned to Joe – 'you watch your manners when you go there, and don't pick up bones like you do here.'

'Mam! they've invited me to tea not a six course dinner.'

'And don't drink out of your saucer,' mimicked Mr Darling, and Joe was forced to burst out laughing.

'You can laugh, the both of you,' said Mrs Darling, busying herself over the meal again. 'But it's manners that count.'

Five minutes later as she placed a plate of bacon and eggs in front of Joe she said, 'And another thing I'll tell you. When you're there, if anybody comes into the room, say a woman like, and you're sitting down you should stand up.'

'What for?'

'Never mind what for; that's what they do.'

'Oh, the Lord preserve us from Westoe and the Richards!' groaned Mr Darling now, looking ceilingwards.

'Well, for your information I knew that afore I went to work at the Richards, so there!' She shook her head at him.

'All right, all right,' said Mr Darling, laughing. 'Ladies, first, last and centre.'

'And that's not always the case either,' said Mrs Darling primly. 'A man should always get off a bus first and help the woman off. And it's the same going into the pictures; he should go first and find the seats and then let her go in.'

When his father pretended to collapse over the table it was too much for Joe. He buried his face in his hands and his shoulders shook with laughter. Then looking up at his mother he said, 'I won't go to tea, Mam; I'll never remember it all and I'll only disgrace you and you'll never be able to lift up your head again in Shields.'

Now his father was bellowing and Mrs Darling

said, 'There's a pair of you. You're as ignorant as pigs, that's what you are . . .'

What with speculation about the solicitor's letter, the trials awaiting Joe, should he go to tea with Anna on Wednesday, the fact that the matter of moving house was settled and that in a week's time they would be living at the other side of the town, the evening passed quickly and Joe didn't think about The Gladiator again until he was in bed; and then it was in a nice sort of way for he could see him in his box next to Ladybird, and surrounded by kindness.

# Twelve

When Joe told Mr Guest, that he would like to be off at half past ten and showed him the letter to verify that his request for absence was genuine, Mr Guest said, 'Well, well! Now this could mean anything. Perhaps they're going to tell you you've had a fortune left you.'

'That'll be the day,' laughed Joe.

'Well, you say you don't know why they want to see you so anything is possible.'

'Aye with prayer and a good wind anything is possible. That's what they say, Sir,' laughed Joe, and he dared to joke. 'So if you're any hand at prayin' you could put in a few for me.'

'Go on with you,' said the master. 'Fortune or no fortune, be back here at quarter to two or you'll have to answer for it.'

'Yes, Sir.' Joe inclined his head, then marched off, feeling both apprehensive and excited.

The door to Peeble & Rice, solicitors, wasn't actually in Fowler Street but in a side street. The building housed a number of offices and Joe had to walk up to the second floor before he saw the names on the glass door. Another door said 'Enquiries' and on this he knocked.

When he was bidden to enter he stopped dead

just inside the room, and his mouth dropped into a gape, because there, standing near a desk, was . . . the man.

'You!' Joe whispered.

'Yes, me,' said Mr Tellman coming forward.

'You a solicitor?'

'No, I'm not a solicitor,' said Mr Tellman; 'I am Mr Peeble's clerk. Take a seat.'

Joe took a seat; his mouth was still open and his eyes were wide. After staring up at Mr Tellman for a moment he said, 'What's it all about? Something to do with The Gladiator?'

'Well, yes, something to do with The Gladiator. You'll know soon enough.'

'But he's all right.'

'Yes, I know he's all right.' Mr Tellman inclined his head. 'Just wait a moment.' And he left Joe and went into another room. It was fully five minutes before he returned, and the five minutes seemed like an hour to Joe because his bewilderment had grown to such proportions that he was in two minds whether to dash out or to sit tight and see what happened. He had never liked that Mr Tellman, never.

'Come this way.' Mr Tellman stood aside and allowed him to pass into another room, and there, one sitting at a desk and one standing with his back to an electric fire, were two old gentlemen. They appeared very old gentlemen to Joe, nearly as old as Mr Prodhurst.

The man at the desk said 'Good morning. Please take a seat.'

And again Joe sat down on the extreme edge of a chair. He looked from the man at the desk to the man at the fireplace; and the man at the fireplace smiled at him widely and said, 'So you're Mr Joseph Darling.'

'Yes, Sir.'

'I'm Mr Rice, and this is Mr Peeble.' The man indicated his partner, then added, 'And you already know our Mr Tellman.'

Joe looked at the man. Yes, he knew him all right.

'Have you any idea why you are here?' asked Mr Rice now, and Joe said quietly, 'No, Sir, not a notion.'

'Not a notion,' repeated Mr Peeble. 'Then didn't our Mr Tellman give you any indication?' He held out his hand towards the man and Joe said, 'Him? I mean . . . Oh no. No, Sir; he just kept coming to the stable. I thought he was to do with the R.S.P.C.A. or some animal concern.'

'So I understand,' said Mr Peeble. 'Well now, I think we have a surprise for you.'

'You have?' said Joe.

'Yes, we have,' said Mr Peeble. 'Although we have been worried over the past fortnight in case you might do something prematurely and then not be in a position to receive the surprise.'

'Oh!' said Joe.

'You don't understand yet. We must make this clear.'

'Well, let's do it,' said Mr Rice moving impatiently from the fire. 'The boy looks so bewildered he thinks he's going to be hanged.' And he now turned to Joe and said, 'It's all right, it's all right. Take the worried look off your face, boy; you've been left some money.'

'What, me!'

'What, me!' repeated Mr Rice looking over the top of his glasses. 'Yes, you.'

'It is this way,' put in Mr Peeble soothingly, and apparently ignoring his partner. 'You were a very good friend to Mr Prodhurst during the latter part of his life.'

'I only knew him for a few months,' said Joe.

'Long enough to make him alter his will in your favour.'

'Mr Prodhurst had a will?'

'Yes, Mr Prodhurst had a will; you could say Mr Prodhurst was very comfortably off.'

'Look,' said Mr Rice; 'read it to the boy. Read it to the boy.'

'All in good time,' said Mr Peeble, still patiently; then drawing the paper towards him he said, 'Three weeks before Mr Prodhurst died he called upon us and desired that his will should be changed and in your favour. But there were conditions. I will read you a letter from his own hand.' Mr Peeble now lifted up a piece of paper, held it at some distance from him and began to read:

'This is to state that I am in my right mind and want to change my will in favour of the boy, Joseph Darling. This boy came into my life a few months ago and has brought me comfort and company and has proved to me, what I very often doubted, that folks could be kind without any hope of reward. Apart from my horse I have had very little companionship for many a long year until I made the acquaintance of this young lad. Perhaps this is my own fault. Well now, I've got a feeling on me that my time's running out. If things had happened that I hadn't met this young lad, I would have called upon Mr Billings to put my animal down, but as it is this boy has taken a fancy to The Gladiator, as I call him, and The Gladiator to him. My horse is an intelligent creature, old as he is, and he doesn't take to everybody, so I'm going to leave the animal to the boy, together with a sum of six pounds. Now six pounds won't go very far these days, not to keep an animal, and then there'll be the rent. If I'm right in judging this boy's character he'll find a way to keep The Gladiator alive. If he does this he'll have his reward. If I should have been mistaken then it'll be his loss. This is what I want you to do, Mr Peeble. I don't want you to give the boy any inkling of what's in store for him, but if he still has the horse in his possession two months from the date of my death then he is to have all the money that is deposited between the two Building Societies here mentioned and the Westminster Bank. If, however, he has disposed of the horse before that time I wish you to give him five pounds for every day the horse has been in his possession. This is my wish.

Signed Edward George Prodhurst.'

'There,' said Mr Peeble. 'What do you think of that?'

Joe's mouth was open. He closed it, then opened it again, and his voice was a mere whisper when he said, 'I don't rightly know.' Then he looked at Mr Tellman, and Mr Peeble said, 'Mr Tellman was quite concerned for you in case you sold the horse or let it be put down. He came round on his own, not by our persuasion, although we were aware of his visits. He didn't indicate anything to you, did he?'

'No, Sir.' Joe swallowed and reddened slightly as he thought how he had disliked Mr Tellman. In some way it was the case of Harry Farthing all over again. You couldn't judge people on appearance or how they acted first go off. And Mr Prodhurst was going to give him five pounds for every day he kept The Gladiator. Five pounds every day! He must have had a bit of money.

'Are you wondering how much you have inherited?' now asked Mr Peeble.

'Tell the boy, tell the boy. Keeping him on hot bricks like this!' Mr Rice now turned to Joe and, bending over him, he said slowly, his voice now no longer irritable, but very kind, 'Mr Prodhurst left you two thousand three hundred and fifty-five pounds, boy.'

Joe stared into the long grey looking face of Mr Rice and then he knew he was going to be sick.

He didn't know which one of them whipped him up by the collar and pushed him into the cloakroom, but it was Mr Tellman who handed him a towel and said, 'There now, there now. It's all right; it was the shock.'

They gave him a glass of water, and then from another room Mr Tellman brought a tray with three cups of coffee on it, and when he had drunk the hot coffee he felt a bit better and his head cleared, and he looked from one to the other of the men and said, 'I'm sorry for that.'

'It's all right, it's all right.' They were all solicitous. 'It was the shock,' said Mr Peeble.

Joe gazed up at the faces looking down at him, and he said softly, 'I thought he was poor.'

'He was a very careful man,' said Mr Peeble.

'His wants were few. He didn't make a fortune, but what he did make he saved.'

Now Joe asked a question that puzzled the three of them, 'Why,' he said, 'when he could have been comfortable?'

When they didn't answer he said, 'It was an awful room, no comfort, nothin'.'

'Apparently he didn't need material comforts,' said Mr Rice, 'and you made his last days happy. I'm sure you would like to have this letter.'

Joe took the letter, but when he looked down at the writing all the words ran into one. Mr Prodhurst . . . Mr Prodhurst had left him all that money; over two thousand pounds. He had left over two thousand pounds to him. If he thought about it too much he'd be sick again, and cry into the bargain.

'The two months was up last Friday night,' said Mr Tellman now. 'I was very relieved when the snow stopped you from sending the animal away, but as it turned out it would still have been all right because you were only having him stabled elsewhere so to speak. I told Mr Peeble and Mr Rice you were prepared to pay for him, weren't you?'

'Oh yes.' Joe nodded at the two solicitors, and Mr Rice said, 'Where were you going to find the money?'

'Well, I got fifteen shillings a week pocket money and me mam was helping me with the rest.'

Mr Peeble now walked towards his desk, saying, 'Mr Prodhurst was a very astute man, indeed, indeed. Well now.' He turned and confronted Joe. 'Would you like our advice on how to use the money?'

'Yes, please, Sir.' Joe nodded.

'We have discussed the matter already, Mr Rice and myself that is.' He nodded towards his partner. 'First of all, we know that you will keep the animal for the rest of its life, and we would advise you to invest the two thousand pounds. This should bring you in at least eighty pounds a year free of tax, and this sum should cover the horse's needs. Then there is the three hundred and fifty-five pounds. Doubtless there are lots of things you would like to buy out of this sum, but still we would advise you to invest part of it, in such a way that you could call on it at any time that was necessary. But of course, of course—' Mr Peeble now waved his hand – 'you will want to discuss this matter with your parents, and anyway this is all subject to your parents signing for the legacy on your behalf as you are under age. It's a matter of formality, you understand?'

Joe didn't quite but he nodded and said he did. 'Nevertheless,' – Mr Peeble now lifted his finger and wagged it at Joe – 'we would strongly advise them not to suggest that you break into the two thousand as long as the animal is alive, because once you use your capital you would still have to find the money to keep the horse. Now we know you would do this but we would advise you to remain firm against any other advice you might get regarding this matter, and keep the two thousand pounds intact until such time as the animal is no longer your responsibility.'

'Yes, Sir.' Joe nodded at Mr Peeble. 'I see your point, an' I will. No matter what anybody says I'll put it in the Bank or, as you say, invest it.'

'You would be very wise,' said Mr Peeble. 'And

if you wish we will act for you. You have just to call on us, hasn't he, Mr Rice?'

'Yes, yes, of course,' said Mr Rice.

Joe now looked at the old men, and they were old men, and they talked old-like, precise and old-like, but they were nice, and wise ... and he wished he didn't feel sick.

'Now you'll want to dash home and tell your parents the good news,' said Mr Peeble, and Joe, getting to his feet, said, 'Yes, Sir. And thank you. Thank you all.'

He turned now to Mr Tellman and, looking up in his face, he said, 'I'm sorry if I was roughish, I mean rude. I didn't mean to be but ... but I thought you were after The Gladiator, to have him put down or somethin'.'

Mr Tellman laughed outright now and Mr Rice joined in, and so did Mr Peeble; then Mr Peeble said, 'Mr Tellman was greatly concerned for you. Mr Tellman has our clients' welfare at heart as much as we have.'

They all went through the outer office and stood on the landing as he went down the stairs, and when Joe reached the street he thought it was very different from what he had seen on the pictures. Sharp-shooting solicitors with swanky offices.

He now looked at the sky, then up Fowler Street, and down Fowler Street. He was in a daze. This couldn't be him. He had come from the college wondering what trouble was facing him and now he was going back with a fortune behind him. Well, it was a fortune, two thousand three hundred and fifty-five pounds, and all because he chatted to Mr Prodhurst and went for his medicine. Mr Prodhurst didn't even know that he was giving him a Christmas box, or that his mam was making him a cake and things, and yet he had left him all his money. It was funny but he still felt sick, not elated or anything.

As he walked up the steep street he thought, It'll pass, the feeling, will pass. And gradually it did.

He had entered Westoe, when he stopped and said, 'What am I doing, going back to the college at half past twelve? I must be going up the pole. I must go and tell me mam.'

He had turned about and hurried homewards before he realized that his mother wouldn't be in. She'd be at the Richards working. He stopped in the street again. Should he go to the Richards? Eeh! no! He'd better not. She had always told him not to come round there because she didn't want Mrs Richards to think she was passing anything on to him. Because that was the way it was done, getting the bairns to go round and stuffing their pockets before they left.

And there was no chance of seeing his dad, for he worked over the river and he certainly couldn't get over there and back before quarter to two.

He knew what he'd do; he'd go and have a slap-up meal somewhere. It was only when he thrust his hand into his trouser pocket and pulled out the half-a-crown that his mother had given him for his dinner in the college restaurant that he knew that the slap-up dinner was off an' all. He started to laugh gently to himself. There was nothing for it; he'd have to go back to the college if he wanted to eat at all.

It was as he entered the grounds that a spurt of

glee came into him as he thought, I'll tell Willie. He won't believe it, but still I'll tell him.

And Willie didn't believe it. He said, 'Oh aye? Pull the other one, lad; it's got bells on.'

'Oh all right then,' said Joe nonchalantly. 'But where do you think I've been this morning? I had to ask off, hadn't I?'

Willie now began to think. Joe could almost see the wheels turning in his mind. Then Willie said, 'But that lousy old bloke . . .'

Before he could get any further Joe came at him, grinding out between his teeth, 'He wasn't a lousy old bloke, he was clean, a jolly sight cleaner than you are sometimes. He lived like that because he wanted to live like that, but he needn't have. He had money behind him and' – Joe now emphasized each word with a dip of his head – 'he left-it-all-to-me . . . and his horse.'

They were in the practical lab and now Willie, supporting himself against the bench, wagged his jaw twice before he said, 'I can't believe it.'

'Well—' Joe jerked his head – 'you're believing it quicker than I did; I was sick.' He laughed. 'They had to take me out because I was sick. It was the shock.'

This last item of news definitely convinced Willie that Joe wasn't having him on, but he did not evince any pleasure. His face quite straight now, he said, 'And all for looking after a mouldy horse! All right, all right—' he flapped his hand at Joe – 'don't tell me again that it wasn't mouldy. It was a racehorse; it could have won The National; you were the envy of everybody in the town.'

Joe now stared at his friend, because no matter

how they disagreed Willie was his friend, and he thought, I may not have been the envy of the people in the town because I owned The Gladiator but this one bloke envies me now.

The knowledge brought no pleasure to Joe. He had known that Willie wouldn't believe him right away but he'd thought that when he did he would have slapped him on the back. But people were funny; they never did what you expected them to do. He should know that by now. Look at Harry Farthing and Mr Tellman. Oh aye, Mr Tellman.

He went to his bench and it was about half an hour later when Mr Guest came up to him, 'What's this I'm hearing, Joe?'

'Oh.' Joe looked up. 'Willie Styles been telling you, Sir?'

'Yes, yes. Is it true though that the old man left you his money, over two thousand pounds?'

'Aye, it's true, Sir.'

'Well, well! Talk about the luck of the devil.' Mr Guest wagged his head. 'And all because you looked after his horse.'

'Yes,' said Joe flatly; 'an' all because I looked after his horse, Sir.'

'I suppose you'll go on a spending spree now?'

'No, Sir; I have no intention of going on a spending spree.'

'No?'

'No. I'm going to invest the money.' Joe's chin was well up and out. He almost added, 'On the advice of my solicitor,' but that would have been a bit too much, he thought.

'You're full of surprises, Joe.'

Joe said nothing to this, but when Mr Guest tapped him appreciatively on the shoulder before moving on he thought, I'm not the only one.

It was a different Willie who accompanied Joe out of the college, and before they had gone very far Joe was given the reason.

'Wouldn't you like to go halves with me m . . . m . . . motor bike?' asked Willie off-handedly.

'How much have you got towards it?' asked Joe, slanting a glance up at him.

'Well . . . well.' Willie hedged. 'I haven't started saving up yet, but what I was thinking was I could sort of borrow the money and could pay it back like on the instalment plan . . .'

'You can save your breath, Willie; I'm not goin' in for any motor bike and I'm not lending you the money.'

'Who asked you?'

'You did. Anyway, most of my money . . .' That had a nice sound. 'Most of my money'll be tied up for some years. I'll only have a bit to play about with, and I've got a lot to do with that. And what's more I've never had a fancy for a motor bike. A car, yes, and as soon as I'm seventeen I'll get one. But as regards the motor bike, I'm not interested, man, but I'll give you a treat somewhere. We'll talk about it the morrow; I've got to get home now.'

At this, Willie visibly brightened and was quick with a suggestion. 'What about g . . . g . . . going and see Newcastle play on Saturday?'

'Aye, a good idea,' said Joe.

'See you the morning then,' said Willie.

'Aye,' said Joe. 'Good night.'

'Good night,' said Willie.

Their ways had just parted when Willie turned round and shouted, 'Joe!'

'Aye? What is it?'

'I'm glad about the money, man. I am.'

'OK.' said Joe. 'OK.' He felt happy of a sudden, and he dashed up all the side streets he knew because he couldn't wait to get home quickly enough.

There was one thing certain, he knew what his mam's and dad's immediate reaction would be: they'd be over the moon. There was no doubt about that. He meant to buy his mam a spanking present; and his dad too. Oh yes, he'd have to get his dad something nice, perhaps something for the car. And his gran . . . He was running when he thought of his gran, and he stopped. They were moving on Friday. She'd know nothing about it until the van was at the door. It wasn't right somehow. He wasn't happy about it. As he had said, it was a dirty way to do things. But then there was the question of his mam's and dad's happiness. It was either one or the other it seemed; stay in Mabel Street and separate, or go down to James Street and continue as a family.

He started to run again, and as he ran he thought of Anna. If Mr Prodhurst had known how she was to work for The Gladiator he would have mentioned her an' all, so it would be up to him to see she got something nice. He would have to ask her mother and father on the quiet what she wanted. And then he would like to buy something for Mrs Billings because she had been so kind with the bits and pieces . . . And then there was Harry Farthing and that twenty-one shillings he had collected. He would slip Harry a fiver on the quiet. He'd like doing that. Oh, he had a lot to do, lots to think about.

He came to his own back lane and sprinted up it, burst through the back door, up the yard, then he was in the kitchen and standing looking at his mother and father and his grannie.

His grannie was crying. The tears were washing all over her face. She was shaking her head from side to side and his dad was yelling at her, 'How did you ferret this out? I knew this would happen that's why I didn't tell you.'

'I ferreted nothing out, lad.' Her voice was broken. 'She came at dinner time. I was at my front door. She was just looking at your window; she was wondering if her curtains would fit; she had forgotten . . . forgotten to ask you.'

Joe looked at his mother. She was standing, still in her outdoor things, opposite the banked-down fire. She had her two hands above her head gripping the high mantelpiece.

Now he watched his grannie look towards his mother and speak directly to her in that awful, heart-breaking, cracked voice. 'Mona,' she said; 'don't do it. For God's sake, lass, don't do it. Don't leave me here on me own. I won't die, I'll just go mad. I'm sorry for all I've done to you, but I haven't known where I've been since Harry went. I've been so lonely and lost. I should have known better, I shouldn't have interfered. Lass, if you'll only stay I'll promise you afore God I'll never trouble you again. I'll never come down into this house unless I'm asked, only don't move, don't leave me here with not a soul of me own near me. You're all I've got, you and him and the lad. I might not have acted as if I've appreciated you, but it's been jealousy, pure and simple, jealousy. I knew you were a good wife. I was jealous of your happiness. That's the top and bottom of it. But don't, don't leave me, lass.'

As his grannie's voice trailed away Joe thought he couldn't bear it. He wanted to fly to her and say, 'It's all right, Gran, it's all right.' He even wanted to say, 'I'll stay with you.' And then his father was barking again, 'It's too late in the day for that, Mother. You should have thought about this a year ago. Aye, two years ago. You've played us up and now you've got to take the consequences. It's too late; the people are ready for moving, the same as us . . . We've all got to get used to being alone some day or other and . . .'

'Be quiet a minute.' Joe watched his mother turn slowly about and look at his grannie. She was crying too, a slow quiet crying. The two women were staring at each other, looking at each other as they had never done during all their acquaintance deep into each other's eyes, and beyond; and then his mother said quietly, 'It's all right.' And his gran said, 'Aw, lass.' And his dad bellowed, 'What do you mean, it's all right? Look, we're going. Who's going to tell those people? I'm not going to be made a laughing stock of . . . Look, what's come over you? You've been breaking your neck to get away. I've done this because of you, and now you tell her it's all right, why? WHY?'

Now his mother was shouting, and at his dad. 'Because I'm not dead yet. I've got a long way to go. It's just come to me, that. That's true; I've got a long way to go. And because there might come the day when I've got to stand there and beg him—' now she was thrusting her hand towards Joe – 'to go on living below me because . . . because I want his company.'

Mr Darling made no retort to this, he just stared at his wife for a long moment. Then after drooping his head he sat down heavily on a chair and said weakly, 'But what are we going to do, it's all fixed?'

'Leave that to me. I'll go down and tell them.' Mrs Darling again looked at her mother-in-law, who was gripping the back of a chair with both hands, and she said to her quietly, 'It's all right. Don't frash yourself anymore.'

'You'll never regret it, lass. You'll never regret it. I promise you, as God's me jud . . .' She choked on her words.

'I know, I know, so don't worry. Sit yourself down and I'll make a cup of tea.'

'Thanks all the same, lass, but I'll go on up.'

His grannie had reached the door when Joe, heaving his voice over the lump that was blocking his gullet, cried, 'Don't . . . don't go for a minute, Gran; I've . . . I've got something to tell you. It's good news. I want you to hear it. Sit down, sit down.' He went towards her and gently led her back to a chair, and when she was seated he looked at his mother and father. Then swallowing deeply, he said, 'I've . . . I've come into money.'

'You've what!' Mr Darling brought his head poking forward. 'You've come into what?'

'Dad, don't keep repeating. You're not deaf, you heard . . . money.'

His mother now had hold of him by the arm. Her face was still wet with her crying, but she smiled as she said, 'The solicitor's letter?'

'Aye, Mam, aye. An' you'd better sit down because you might be like me, you might fall down when I tell you.'

They sat, the three of them, and he looked at them and he let a few seconds pass before he said, 'Mr Prodhurst left me all his money because I looked after The Gladiator. If I had let him go like everybody was telling me to I wouldn't have got it, except five pounds a day for as long as I kept him. It was in his will: I had to hang on to him for two months and then I would have all his money.'

'Old Ted with money?' His father's statement implied utter disbelief.

'Aye, Dad, money, real money.'

'How much?' asked his mother practically.

Joe allowed another few seconds to pass before he said, 'Two thousand three hundred and fifty-five pounds.'

There was a much longer pause before his mother exclaimed below her breath, 'You're joking, boy.' She had her hands on her stomach and he knew she was feeling the same as he did when he got the shock. He took after her in that way; any upset and the first place it registered was in his stomach.

When they continued to stare at him without speaking he looked from one to the other and asked on a high note, 'Well, aren't you going to say anything? Aren't you pleased? . . . By! folks are funny.'

'Pleased?' His father was on his feet now, thumping him on the back. 'Pleased, lad? I'm staggered.'

His mother was standing in front of him, holding his two hands, shaking them up and down as she kept repeating, 'Joe. Oh Joe.'

His grannie didn't say anything. She was crying again worse than ever, but going to her now he put his hand gently on her shoulder and shook it, saying, 'If you keep your nose clean, Gran. I'll buy you a packet of bullets,' whereupon she put her arms swiftly round him and held him to her, and as he returned her embrace he thought, Now I can enjoy it because it wouldn't have been the same if we had done the dirty on her.

It had been a hectic evening, a suitable end to a surprising and hectic day.

The clock in the sitting-room was chiming twelve and he was still wide awake. Earlier in the evening he had gone round to Anna's to tell her the news; he just couldn't wait until tomorrow when he was due to go to tea.

The Billings family had reacted very much like his own people. They had been over the moon for him. But at one point Mr Billings had become very grave, and he had covered his face for a moment before he said, 'And had you taken my advice you would have had the poor animal put to sleep. Well, it just goes to show, you should never try to persuade anybody against their will, especially if they feel they're doing the right thing. It was a very narrow squeak, Joe.'

Joe had nodded as if he were agreeing with Mr Billings, but he didn't see it as a narrow squeak, because right from the start he had been determined to hang on to The Gladiator as long as possible.

It was Anna who asked, 'Have you told Matty and Mr Walsh?' and when he had said, 'No, not yet; I'm going to phone them when I leave,' Mrs Billings had said, 'Do it from here, now.' And he had done just that. He had got on the phone, and

Mrs Walsh had answered, and he had told her and laughed aloud as she squealed her excitement. And then she had called her husband, and Mr Walsh had said, 'Well now, cast thy bread on the waters and it will be returned to you a thousandfold. Well, boy, you threw out a straw and you got a bale of hay back in this case.' And Joe laughed and said 'Aye, Mr Walsh, the equivalent like, any rate.' Then Mr Walsh said, 'You'll have no need for a helping hand to keep The Gladiator now. I'll have to see about putting up my charges, won't I?' And Joe had laughed and said, 'An' you can do that an' all, Mr Walsh.'

Then Matty was on the line, his tone from his first few words expressing his pleasure at the luck that had befallen his friend, and when he said, 'It couldn't have happened to a nicer bloke, Joe,' Joe's face flushed and, looking at Anna, who was standing by his side listening, he whispered, 'He's daft.'

And Anna, glancing towards Joe with a twinkle in her eye, called into the phone, 'He's not bad at times, Matty, but he's nicer to horses than he is to people.' Whereupon Joe's face went redder still.

Going back over the evening he didn't know when he had enjoyed himself more, or felt more happy. And his cup was full when, reaching home, he saw his mam and dad and grannie sitting down to supper together.

His dad had chaffed him about Anna, and his mam had said, 'Did you mind your manners?' And his grannie had said, 'What does he need manners for when he's got over two thousand pounds?' and they all laughed uproariously.

It had been a grand evening, grand. Life was

grand. It was stretching before him filled with excitement, and all because of The Gladiator . . . Aye, and Mr Prodhurst. He wished he could see Mr Prodhurst for just a minute to let him know how he felt, say thank you, sort of, but perhaps he knew. Aye, perhaps he did. He conjured the old man's face up before him, he saw the bushy untidy whiskers, the wrinkles round his deep-set blue eyes, the thin hair smoothed across his forehead, and his mouth, his big, kind, generous mouth. He saw him laughing as he used to when they sat opposite each other at the table, and he whispered into the darkness. Thanks for everything, Mr Prodhurst.

He now closed his eyes and put his hands behind his head and told himself there was nothing more in the world he wanted. Aw well . . . perhaps just one thing, to be a bit taller, say another few inches, say five foot seven or eight. It would make all the difference because people didn't take you for much if you were small.

At this moment he had the strong impression that he heard Mr Prodhurst laugh; it was a hearty, free kind of laugh, and it filled the bedroom. Then he distinctly heard him say, 'Never you fear, Joe. If you've got to grow you'll grow, but there's one thing certain, nobody will ever take you for anything else but a gladiator.'

THE END

# MATTY DOOLIN

### BY CATHERINE COOKSON

Matty Doolin is fifteen and, in his Tyneside
home in the 1960s, this means it is time for him
to leave school and follow his father into the
docks. All Matty really wants, however, is to
work with animals, tend them, help them, care
for them. But he has no qualifications and his
parents have no real understanding of his ambi-
tion – they won't even let him keep Nelson, the
old stray dog he befriends and takes home.

Yet, finally, it is because of Nelson that Matty
gets permission to go on a camping holiday
with his friends, Joe and Willie. And this
holiday, on a farm high on the fells, is to take
Matty through unexpected danger to a new
and satisfying way of life.

SBN 0 552 52526X

# LANKY JONES

### BY CATHERINE COOKSON

Tall, lanky, Daniel Jones and his father are only too happy to accept an offer of shelter in an isolated farm house when their car gets stuck in a snowdrift, and the two families quickly become firm friends.

But Daniel can sense danger, a weird kind of danger, lurking beneath the surface friendliness. Who is the mystery person screaming in the night? What is making the noises he can hear coming from the disused attic? And why is the unpleasant Billy Combo hanging around all the time? Suddenly Daniel finds himself caught up in a terrifying adventure, his very life at stake . . .

A page-turning tale of courage, danger and excitement

SBN 0 552 521418